VAIM

Jon Fosse was born in 1959 on the western coast of Norway and is the recipient of countless prestigious prizes, both in Norway and abroad. Since his 1983 fiction debut, *Raudt, svart* [Red, Black], Fosse has written prose, poetry, essays, short stories, children's books and over forty plays. In 2023, he was awarded the Nobel Prize in Literature 'for his innovative plays and prose which give voice to the unsayable'. *Vaim* is his tenth book with Fitzcarraldo Editions.

Damion Searls is a translator from German, Norwegian, French and Dutch, and a writer in English. He has translated twelve books by Jon Fosse, including the three books of *Septology*.

'Jon Fosse is a major European writer.'
— Karl Ove Knausgaard, author of *The Wolves of Eternity*

'The Beckett of the twenty-first century.'
— *Le Monde*

'Fosse's distinctive prose style – a spare, elegant minimalism deftly complicated by stylized, mesmeric repetitions – conjures a suitably haunting atmosphere, a sense of a once familiar world turned uncannily strange.'
— Houman Barekat, *Financial Times*

'Fosse is a great novelist of our time.'
— Rónán Hession, *Irish Times*

'I think the great splendour of Fosse's fiction is that it so deeply rejects any singular interpretation; as one reads, the story does not sound a clear singular note, but rather becomes a chord with all the many possible interpretations ringing out at once. This refusal to succumb to the solitary, the stark, the simple, the binary – to insist that complicated things like death and God retain their immense mysteries and contradictions – seems, in this increasingly partisan world of ours, a quietly powerful moral stance.'
— Lauren Groff, *Guardian*

'He touches you so deeply when you read him, and when you have read one work you have to continue.... What is special with him is the closeness in his writing. It touches on the deepest feelings that you have – anxieties, insecurities, questions of life and death – such things that every human being actually confronts from the very beginning. In that sense I think he reaches very far and there is a sort of universal impact of everything that he writes.'
— Anders Olsson, Nobel committee

Fitzcarraldo Editions

VAIM

JON FOSSE

Translated by
DAMION SEARLS

I

So, I said, well here we are, I said and I ran my fingers through my beard, my greying beard, I wasn't young anymore, no, but I wasn't an old man either, it would probably be fair to say ageing, yes, an ageing man, neither more nor less, and it was about time I stopped taking these little sprees to Bjørgvin, what was the point anymore, tying up at the quay of The Wharf in Bjørgvin and not using my time there to do anything but sit in a bar or restaurant or café, yes, usually The Fowl, that's what they call the place, but sometimes I'd go to The Food Hall or The Last Boat, or The Coffeehouse – other than going somewhere like that or just staying in the cabin of my boat there wasn't really anything to do, or, well, the first day, or first couple of days, there'd be something I needed to buy, yes, always, this or that, there'd be one thing or another that I'd thought might come in handy and I'd written it down on a sheet of paper on my living room table back home, something I couldn't get at The Vaim General Store but that would come in handy, it was always different, it could be anything, yes, over the years I'd gradually bought everything I really needed but a needle and some black thread to sew a loose button back on, yes, that's what I needed to buy this year, but actually it was a lot harder than you'd think to buy a single needle and a single spool of black thread in the city of Bjørgvin, Norway's second biggest city, it was almost unbelievable how hard it was, you'd almost think that the shopkeepers didn't want to bother selling something as small as a needle and spool of thread, because I'd walked from one clothing shop to the next and none of them had anything like that for sale, no, they said, no, we don't carry that, and you'd have to say that there was something a little bit mocking in their answer, and in their face behind that answer, and when I asked where I might be able to buy it the answer was always the same, no, we don't know, sometimes they would add that they don't sell needle and thread in this shop, only clothes, ready-to-wear clothes as they put it, and now if I wanted to buy myself some new clothes, if I could afford it, and I have to admit that one of them, or maybe more than one of them, was hinting that I needed some new clothes, but I didn't need new clothes, I was doing just fine with the clothes I already had, because I didn't look like a beggar or anything, no, even if some people probably thought I did, but these clothing stores were packed with clothes and that was probably the reason for this hinting, and also the reason why they didn't want to sell me a needle and thread, but eventually there was someone standing in front of me, bowing to me, in a suit, dammit if he wasn't wearing a pink tie, who said that if I wanted to buy a needle and a spool of black thread I would need to go to a tailor's, and when I ventured to ask him where I might find a tailor this shopkeeper's assistant, or maybe it was the store owner for all I knew, just laughed, he laughed long and loud with his mouth wide open and said how should he know, and then he said that there always used to be a tailor on Skostredet back in the day, but that was a long time ago, because it's been a long time since there were any tailors in Bjørgvin or probably out on the coast in Strileland either, he said and then a woman came in through a door behind the counter that the man in the suit and pink tie was leaning on and asked a bit impatiently if there was something she could help with and the man in the suit and pink tie said yes, so, um, well, and then I mumbled that I wanted to buy a needle and a spool of black thread and she asked if I needed it to sew a loose button back on and I said yes, that's what I wanted, and she said she could get that for me, yes, and then she disappeared through the door she had just come in through and the man in the pink tie said yes, yes, you see, the things I don't know, the things I can't do, and I asked if he'd just started working in the shop and he said he'd been working there his whole life, since he was a little boy, because the woman who'd just gone to get a needle and thread was his mother, and after his blessed father had died much too young it was Mother, as he put it, yes, she owned the shop, and he had never got any further in life than to work as a shop assistant for his own mother, he said and she was someone who sold anything she could, he could say that for sure, yes, she'd sell her own grandmother if it came to it, yes, that's what they liked to say about enterprising salespeople in Bjørgvin, he said, so now his mother had probably gone upstairs to their apartment to find a needle and some thread in her own sewing kit, it wasn't the first time she'd done that, yes, go get something from the apartment to sell it, that's how his father's wardrobe had disappeared, not all at once of course, it took its time, but eventually everything got sold, so I'd get my needle and thread all right, the man who was also her son said, and then we stood there not saying anything and then the door behind the counter opened and she came in, and she held up a spool of black thread and there was a needle stuck into the thread, I could see it and yes well here you have your needle and thread, she said, the widow, mother, and owner of a clothing shop in Bjørgvin, yes, I have everything anyone might want for sale, she said, with maybe a little pride in her voice, and her son in the suit wearing a pink tie shrugged, and he wasn't exactly young, more like a male old maid by the look of him, but how can I think such a thing, to tell the truth I'm no less of an old maid than he is, probably more of one actually, since it seems like I'm a lot older than the son with the pink tie, but then again I had nothing womanly about me, not at all, but that guy, the son, in the suit, with the pink tie, yes, he was as feminine as he was masculine, and that's probably why I'd hit on that phrase, old maid, yes, and his mother both looked like a man and was acting like one too and she held out her hand with that spool of thread with a needle stuck into it and she said to me

That'll be two hundred and fifty kroner, she said

and I couldn't believe it, two hundred and fifty kroner for a spool of black thread and a needle, yes, everyone knows that these Bjørgvin people sure gouge money out of people but this was above and beyond even for Bjørgvin, this was outrageous, exorbitant, yes that's the word, exorbitant, there's nothing else you can call it, I could buy myself a new shirt for that, several shirts, and avoid the trouble of sewing the button back on too, because it's always a hassle, just getting the thread through the needle always takes me a long time, my eyesight isn't the best, and even my glasses don't help much when it comes to seeing the eye of the needle

Well, the woman standing behind the counter said with a kind of swagger

Well, what'll it be, she said

and I had to just buy that needle and thread from this awful woman, owner of a clothing shop in the city of Bjørgvin, mother of a son in a pink tie, there was probably nothing else I could do, I thought and I took my wallet out of my jacket pocket, but really, no, I couldn't, I couldn't pay that much for a little needle and a little thread on a spool where most of the thread had already been used, yes, as far as I could tell there was only a little thread left on the spool, maybe not even enough to sew a single button on with, no, really, but once you start something you have to finish it, once a person's said A they have to say B, as the saying goes, and if I said no to buying it now it would be kind of humiliating, yes, I'd probably look like a pauper in the eyes of this lady behind the counter, and that's exactly what I didn't want, I didn't want to give her that pleasure, I'd rather she have the somewhat dubious pleasure of having cheated a man, of having cheated a country bumpkin from Strileland even, I thought as I stood there with my wallet in my hand and I took out a two-hundred-kroner note and a fifty and I put them down on the counter, I laid the money down without saying a word and as soon as I put the notes down they were in that woman's hands, and then I stood there like a fool looking at the spool with a needle stuck into what was left of the black thread and she, the owner of this clothing shop in Bjørgvin, didn't say anything and I didn't either, I was glad I wasn't going to give her an answer and her son, in the black suit and the pink tie, where had he gone off to? I looked all around the shop and it was a big and nice shop, I had to admit that, and there, way in the back, in front of a mirror, was the son, grooming himself, running the palm of his hand over his hair, straightening his tie, standing up straight to his full height making himself look as thin as he could and I put the needle and thread in my pocket and thought now, yes, now I've got to get out of this hellish shop, the sooner the better, and I headed for the door without saying a word and behind me I heard the mother and son saying as if with one voice thanks for coming in, hope to see you again, if there's anything else the gentleman needs or wants, thanks for coming in and hope to see you again, I heard behind me, and the words were still echoing in my ears even when I was back out on the streets of Bjørgvin and never again, never again would I set foot in that clothing shop, never, never, I thought, because I'd never been cheated that badly in my whole life probably, I thought, and now I had to get back home to

Vaim, I thought, and why did I always take these boat trips to Bjørgvin anyway, they never really had any point, these excursions, when I had a few days off work then yes I'd just go to Bjørgvin, but it wasn't so often nowadays either, I thought, not for the past few years anyway, yes, for many years now I'd only taken one trip a year on a summer's day even though back when I was younger, yes, back then I would constantly be coming to Bjørgvin, one or two days off and I'd head out, and back then I was a regular customer at the bars, and the reason why was probably that I was hoping, even though I didn't want to admit it, yes, I was hoping to meet someone, yes, someone to share my life with, as they say, but no, not this time, as they say, yes, and now I've got so old that the hope is gone, I'm alone and I'll stay alone, yes, that's how it is on that subject and that's how it'll stay too, yes, so now I took these trips to Bjørgvin just to buy something I couldn't get at The Vaim General Store, but actually there was and is little or nothing I couldn't get at The Vaim General Store, they sell most things, all kinds of things, yes, it was only things like this needle and thread that made me think I'd better go to Bjørgvin to get those, although, strictly speaking, one button more or less didn't matter since really I just putter around and take care of myself in my house, my home, my childhood home as they say, where I was born and where I hope I'll die, the same way both of my parents passed away there, I lived there while they were alive and then after they died too, yes, then I lived there alone, since I was an only child, yes, I've lived in my childhood home my whole life, and now since I live there alone there's no one to see or notice if a button is missing, yes, and if it's a button on my trousers I can always just keep my trousers up with a belt, and I have plenty of belts, or even with some rope if it came to that, which it hasn't, but on the other hand yes you'd have to say it's good to have a needle and thread around, and I'm sure that I have some too, it's just that I forgot where I put it, or, yes, well, it's pretty much certain that it's in the desk drawer where I have my other sewing things that I inherited from my mother, I threw away most of what she left behind, although it took me a while, but the things I could use, like a needle and thread, yes, I kept those, I'm not that big a fool, but, yes, but then why in the world would I go to Bjørgvin to buy a needle and thread even though I most likely had what I needed at home, yes, well, I guess I just thought I should, so actually I was just looking for an excuse to take a little boat trip to Bjørgvin while I was off for the summer and didn't need to go to work, even though maybe I was getting, yes, well, kind of sick of these boat trips, yes, and really it would be nicer if I wasn't always in the boat by myself, there was only one time I had a travelling companion, that's maybe what you call it, and that was when Elias came with me, but that was many years ago now, and also it took years before Elias agreed to come to Bjørgvin with me, I asked him over and over again if he wanted to come but he'd hem and haw and say he was no sailor, he never felt comfortable on the water, but finally, one beautiful summer's day when he dropped by to visit and I mentioned I was taking a boat trip to Bjørgvin he said he'd love to come, sure, and the next day there he was standing outside my house with an old grey rucksack on, and then we walked down to the boat and set out, but he sure wasn't much of a crew, the good man, he got pale after just a little time at sea and he didn't have much talk in him, he just sat there, pale and kind of run-down, then we docked at The Wharf in Bjørgvin and he had a little talk in him, and then I mentioned that we could go drop by The Strileland Liquor Store and he was totally terrified and he said no, no, and that's the only thing I can remember him saying on that whole trip, and so obviously Elias didn't come on the boat with me again, but we drop by each other's house for a visit a lot, yes, he'll look in on me once a week or so or I'll look in on him, in his little house, even though we're so different we stick together, yes, it's fair to say that he's the only friend I have in Vaim, yes, Elias, yes, I don't remember when he came to Vaim and moved into that house but it was many years ago now, and I also don't remember when we met each other and started dropping by each other's house but it was many years ago, and one other thing's for sure, that after that failed trip to Bjørgvin I never asked him again if he wanted to come on the boat with me, we never brought up that whole Bjørgvin trip again, to tell the truth probably neither of us liked to think about it, but anyway it's good that I have Elias to talk to, because there's no one else I see in Vaim, and the part of that trip I remember best is probably the look on Elias's face when I asked him if we should stop by The Strileland Liquor Store, back then I used to stop by there whenever I came to Bjørgvin and buy a bottle or two of whisky, but there was something in Elias's face when I asked him if we should go there that, well, that maybe he wanted to forget, but we never talked about it, so there was no trip to The Strileland Liquor Store that time, and now it's been many years since I've been in there, and it was probably called that because it was on Sea Lane and people from Strileland always used to come to Bjørgvin by boat and tie up at The Wharf, yes, even now that lots of people had their own car there were plenty of people who did that, came to Bjørgvin in their own boat, yes, and most of the people from Strileland bought what they wanted to drink at The Strileland Liquor Store, the ones with their own car too, yes, that's how it was and is, I think and I barely noticed the street I was walking on I was so worked up about having bought that needle and thread, one needle and one barely half-full spool of black thread had cost me two hundred and fifty kroner, but what's done is done, so now I just needed to get back to my boat, my nice little motorboat, and then I needed to get back to Vaim, because I didn't have much to do in Bjørgvin to tell the truth, back in the day, when I was young, just a kid, yes, I would always look forward to these boat trips to Bjørgvin, being in my boat for the hours it took to get to Bjørgvin, and then finding a place to tie up somewhere along The Wharf, yes, and that was kind of exciting too, because especially on summer days there might not be much space along The Wharf, and as for tying up to another boat, tying up to its side facing away from The Wharf, the way some people did when The Wharf was full of boats, no, I've never done that and I never will either, it would feel too crowded, and too aggressive, no, I'd never be able to relax if my boat was tied to another boat, I wouldn't be able to sleep even, I'll be damned if I'd ever cook myself a meal on board, not to mention use the head, no, never, so if there was nowhere to dock along The Wharf I would turn right around and pull slowly out into The Bay and then set my course for the island of Sartor, because there were lots of good harbours out there, with shops on land and nice quays too where you could tie up and spend the night in peace and quiet, yes, my goodness I felt like the best thing to do now would be to just set out from Bjørgvin and head towards Sartor, yes, maybe go to Sund on Sartor, because there was a good quay there, that always had a spot to tie up your boat, and there was a shop there, The Grocery Store, that sold everything you can imagine, yes, maybe even more things than The Vaim

General Store, yes, so if only I'd thought of it I could definitely have bought myself a needle and thread there, and probably for almost nothing, yes, I should think so, and next to The Grocery Store there was also a little house where they'd opened a place to eat, The Tearoom they called it, and they sold coffee and cake there, and you could also buy dinner, but they served only one dish a day, one dinner and one dessert, usually the dinner was meatballs with brown sauce and mashed peas, and the dessert tended to be rice pudding with a red sauce, and that food was nothing to shake a stick at, not at all, and when I was there I usually had meatballs and rice pudding, so maybe, yes, maybe I should leave and go to Sartor today, to Sund, yes, why not really, because actually, and to tell the truth, I had little or nothing left to do in Bjørgvin, the years when I did have things to do here were past, yes, maybe that was the reality, in any case now that I'd let that big-mouthed lady sell me a needle and thread for whatever price she came up with I was a fool, so I should just get out of Bjørgvin, the sooner the better, yes, I should definitely just go right to my boat, yes, with this lousy needle and this damn half spool of thread, and then I should untie the boat and set a course straight to Sartor, to Sund, and I'd buy myself some excellent meatballs and rice pudding at The Tearoom there, I was really and truly looking forward to it, yes, the mere thought of it made me happy, so then it was settled, simple enough, off to Sartor we go, off to Sund we go, that's how it was and I walked a bit faster down the street, yes, not that I had any idea what the street was called, and it didn't matter either, with my spool and my needle in my jacket pocket I walked straight to The Wharf, I wasn't going to let any more Bjørgvin people trick me out of any more money, not on this trip anyway, no, I thought and I went on board and so, I said, so now let's set out and I stopped myself and thought now what do I mean by that, by saying us, because it's just me, I thought, no, no, well, it's me and the boat that make up us, it's me and Eline, and what on earth was it back then that led me to think that I should name my boat Eline, yes, well, I know why, I remember why, but I don't really like to think about it, because Eline, she was the secret love of my youth and it's been a long time now since I got this boat, and back then Eline was probably still my secret love, because I'd never told anybody about that crush, no I don't like that word, but it's probably the exact right word I need to use since there probably isn't any other better word to call it by, to name it, yes, to describe the feelings I had for Eline back then, or maybe there's some other word for it but I never learned it, but it's such a childish word, well be that as it may that's what I called my boat, my motorboat, Eline, and that was even while Eline was still living at home with her parents in Vaim, so what must she have thought, Eline, when she saw the boat tied at The Quay below The Vaim General Store with her name in big letters on both sides of the cabin, yes, Eline probably must have realized that the boat was named after her and it must have made her uncomfortable, yes, she must have been downright embarrassed and thought wasn't that shameless of me to use her name and just go ahead and name my boat after her even though we had hardly ever spoken, so what did that mean, she must have thought, yes, it must mean I'd fallen in love with her, no, how embarrassing, and why would I of all the young men in Vaim do that, that's what she must have thought, yes, something like that, and I can still remember being moored at The Quay below The Vaim General Store and being in the cabin and when I slipped out from behind the curtain I saw Eline standing there with some other young people and they were pointing, without saying a word, first at the nameplate on the boat and then at Eline and then they laughed and guffawed and made fun of both me and my boat, that was what they were doing, and Eline, yes, well, she was standing there laughing too, so of course I cringed in shame and it took a long time before I dared to come out of the cabin and back onto land, that's for sure and certain, but not long after that Eline moved away from Vaim, I didn't know why, but probably to start a job somewhere, and since then I hadn't seen her, but even so many years later I still felt so close to her, yes, it almost felt like I was back in my younger years, but it couldn't be true that I still felt the same for Eline as I did in those bygone days, back then, no, that would be impossible, my feelings for the boat can't help but be mixed in now, because there I was standing in the Eline's cabin, again, like I've done hundreds, yes, thousands of times before, and the motor was purring and running and the boat was gliding with proud dignity out into The Bay, the water was almost perfectly calm and the sky was light blue with some fair-weather clouds for the sun to hide behind and now I left Bjørgvin behind, just let it be, and I'll be damned if I knew when the next time was I'd go back to Bjørgvin, on the boat Eline, most likely never, I thought and the thought did me good, because in that case maybe the humiliation I'd suffered today, when I'd had a needle and thread foisted off on me for a totally shameful price, would lead to something good, it would be best if it did, of course, I thought and the boat glided in stately fashion out into The Bay, out into Bjørgvin Fjord, now I feel good, I thought, this is a fine, sturdy boat, built by a boatbuilder in Strandebarm, the one with the best reputation, Aga was his name, and the boat was twenty-seven feet long, the cabin had a head up in the bow behind a door, and a hole in the ceiling for daylight, and, yes, to air it out, there was a skylight in the cabin too, and other than that there were two berths on each side, and a long narrow table in the middle, there were cupboards on the wall of the cabin between the cabin and the wheelhouse, and if you went through the cabin door you'd be in the wheelhouse, with a captain's wheel and a good chair to sit in on the starboard side, and under that there was even a sink you could pump water up into from a tank all the way in the bow, behind the head, you just had to pull the captain's chair out of the way and you could see the sink in all its glory, and on the port side there was the galley, two hotplates with a kerosene burner, and underneath was the cupboard with shelves for plates and bowls and knives and forks and food and whatever else needed to be stored there, another cupboard with shelves was under the sink on the starboard side, yes, and in the middle was the engine box, where the loyal engine did its trusty work, it always started, and ran steadily, and on summer days like this one it was nice to sit in the fresh air, because at the stern there was the rudder, and there was a space underneath that too where the fuel tank was, and benches to sit on there too, on both sides and at the stern, and there were nice cushions, yes, both on the berths in the cabin and on the captain's chair and on the benches in back, and everything was always in good repair, an oil change and a new filter in the engine every spring, and a diesel filter of course, woodwork coated with boat tar, everything on board the ship was maintained just as well as could be, yes, it was an excellent boat, it was probably just the thing with the name that had gone wrong but there was nothing to be done about that since changing a boat's name was bad luck, I wasn't much of a sailor but I knew that much, and this boat made me so happy, yes, I'd had it for so many years now and spent so many happy hours, yes, days, and nights too, on that boat, I couldn't even count them, no, but if the weather was good for a boat ride I went for one, that's how it was, yes, me and the Eline, yes, you'd have to say we were as close as an old married couple, and I'd even heard people say that, it wasn't the kind of opinion I should have to hear people say but a few guys were standing on The Quay below The Vaim General Store, the way they tended to do, they were in the habit of gathering there, especially when the Bjørgvin ship came in, yes, they were curious, about who was coming ashore and who was going on board, and maybe that was the only exciting thing the boat could bring, or bring to Vaim at least, or else it was probably just an old habit that made them stand there, they wanted to hear the news, the gossip, argue about politics, yes, really just talk and be with other people, and so one day when I was pulling in the group of guys was standing there, of course I knew where they tended to be and I tended to avoid tying up there but for whatever reason I tied up there on that day while they were standing there, I forget why, and then, as I was tying a mooring line, I heard someone say here comes Jatgeir with his old lady, and another guy said yeah, him and Eline, and then all the men had a good laugh, I've often thought about whether they meant for me to hear what they said, actually I don't think they did, no, I don't want to think any more about it, because one thing's for sure and certain that there's no woman I'm closer to than I am to this boat, to the motorboat Eline, and I laid my hand flat on a board of the boat and gently rubbed my hand back and forth along the board and then I sat there and I sort of half-dozed off and Eline glided slowly and carefully over the still water and my thoughts calmed down, and of course the motorboat was named after her, Eline, and she was just a girl when she left home, anyway she was gone from Vaim one day all of a sudden, and a few years later I heard, it must have been at The Vaim General Store, that she'd got married and moved to Sartor, I'd heard she'd found herself a fisherman, but that was many years ago already, I can't remember how many years, and of course it was a stupid idea to name the boat after Eline, but I'd probably heard that a boat should have a female name, and since the name Eline was the one that was constantly spinning around in my head, yes, the boat got named Eline, Eline the person had already been on my mind for several years, often to the point where it was hard to stop thinking about her, yes, and so that's how the boat got named Eline, and there was a lot of talk going around about that name, yes, that's what Elias told me, yes, apparently it was so bad that some people called me Eline instead of Jatgeir, there's Eline, they said when they saw me, and when Elias told me that yes well I didn't ask any more questions, that was just the way it was going to be on that subject, there was nothing I could do about it anyway, that's how it was, and well it was nice that Elias dropped by to see me every now and then, he was the only person who did, and he was the only person I ever dropped by and visited either and now I can already see the bay there at Sund, blue, sparkling, and there are no boats tied up at the quay, and that's good, because then it'll be easy to tie up there, and up on the shore stood The Grocery Store with the name written in big black letters on a white background on the side of the building so you could see it from a long way off, and The Tearoom was written in letters at least as big on the wall of the smaller building next door, so now I'd reached Sund, no doubt about it, and with no wind and no current it couldn't be easier to pull in and tie up the boat and then I let the engine run and cool down for a while before I turned it off, and it sure was nice how it was so quiet everywhere, the water was dead calm, there was not a sound, and I opened the cabin door and went in, left the door open, and then I lay down at full length on the berth, the starboard one, because that was the berth I always used and always had used since I got Eline and then I stretched out my feet and it felt good, so good, to get away from Bjørgvin, so good to tie up the boat on Sartor, in Sund, and now I'd just rest a little and then I'd go ashore and take a walk, stop in at The Grocery Store, I could always buy some food, something small, and it was always good to fill up the fuel tank, and I'd tied up so that the hose from the pump on the quay could easily reach my boat, and in Sund, yes, actually everywhere on Sartor that I could stock up on fuel it was cheaper than in Bjørgvin, yes, cheaper than in Vaim for that matter, so I'd bunker the diesel fuel and then I'd make dinner, I'd fry up some bacon and eggs and potatoes for dinner like always, but maybe today, since I was moored at the Sund quay, I should go to The Tearoom and buy myself some meatballs, because of course they always had meatballs at The Tearoom, sometimes they'd have something else on the menu too but you could buy meatballs every day anyway, and they were good, so maybe I'd splurge a little today and enjoy some meatballs at The Tearoom, or maybe not today, since this was the day I'd been a country bumpkin and let a lady from Bjørgvin swindle me out of two hundred and fifty kroner, embarrassing is what it was, yes, it's almost like the Bjørgvin people were totally justified in looking down on the Strileland people if something like this could happen, but of course I wasn't a Strileland person in the strict sense of the word, even if I tended to call myself one, I was a Sygnefjord person, and Sygnefjord people weren't considered Strileland people, the same way Hardanger people weren't considered Strileland people, it was only the people who lived on islands and on the coast in the surrounding countryside closest to Bjørgvin who were considered and called Strileland people, but I thought of myself as a Strileland person because then at least that meant you weren't a Bjørgvin person, you were the opposite of a Bjørgvin person, while Bjørgvin people could only exist so to speak in opposition to Strileland people, so I thought of myself as a Strileland person, and called myself one, but on Sartor, in Sund, they were all real Strileland people, and that was good, because here you could buy a needle and thread without anyone cheating the life out of you and by god I'd try it, because there, at The Grocery Store, they sold all sorts of things, groceries of course, and other daily items, but also clothes, ready-to-wear clothing they called it, and also yarn, paint, anything you could imagine, yes, so they most likely also had spools of black thread and needles you could use to sew buttons back on with, yes, anyway I could ask for that there at The Grocery Store, and now I've probably lain down and had a rest for long enough so it's time to get up and get something done and the tide was as high as it gets so it was easy to climb up onto the old floating deck hanging off the side of the quay and get up onto the quay, and once I was up on land I looked around, and it was nice here in Sund, buildings and houses arranged prettily around the bay, and if you looked out at the water the approach from Bjørgvin was there to the northeast, and if you looked southeast, yes, then you'd see the inlet, the *sund*, that gave the place its name, and then the lovely row of boathouses down there on the shore, boathouse after boathouse, and dock after dock, yes, it was nice in Sund, but now I should probably go to The

Grocery Store and ask them if they had a spool of black thread for sale, and a needle I could use to sew a loose button back on with, I thought and I slid open the front door of The Grocery Store, I'd been there so many times before, and it didn't look like there were any other customers there, and there, over by one of the shelves with things for sale, there was The Shopkeeper, she wasn't exactly young, and I'd probably seen her at The Grocery Store many times before, not that I could remember it, maybe she was the owner of the store and I just went straight over to her and asked her if she had black thread and a needle for sewing a button on with and she looked closely at me, examined me up and down for a long time, it seemed to me, and then she said yes, sure, a needle and thread to sew a button on with, they had that, imagine if everyone from Sund had to go all the way to Bjørgvin to get their loose buttons sewn back on, wouldn't that be something, yes, she said and I nodded and said that I heartily agreed, so true, so true, and then The Shopkeeper said that I should follow her and she'd find a needle and thread for me, now come with me, she said and she walked through the store past several shelves where all kinds of things for sale were on display in tidy rows, and then she disappeared around the end of one of the shelves, and I hurried to catch up, I turned the corner around the shelf and bumped right into The Shopkeeper's backside, because she'd stopped, and she was standing there looking for something with her arms reaching up high into the air, and then she brought one of her arms down, held out her hand, and in it was a spool of black thread

This should do it, she said

and she handed me the spool of thread and I took it and this spool of thread was even wrapped in plastic, so at least it hadn't been used, unlike the one I'd bought from the lady in Bjørgvin

Looks fine, I said

I should think so, The Shopkeeper said

and then she said now she had to find the right kind of needle, one with an eye big enough that I'd be able to thread it, she said, and they had needles in various sizes so she should probably be able to find a good one, she said and I didn't say anything and just stood there and saw her pull a drawer out and then she looked at various needles and handed me a needle

Is this good? she said

and I said yes I would say so, the needle wasn't so big that it wouldn't fit through any hole it needed to go through, and the eye was big enough that even I wouldn't have any trouble getting the thread through it, I said, so it's perfect, I said, I'll take it, both needle and thread, I said and then The Shopkeeper turned around and walked, and it was, yes, how should I put it, yes, a queenly walk, maybe I could put it that way, she went over to the counter and the cash register and stood behind the counter and entered the total and then she said that'll be two hundred and fifty kroner, and I couldn't believe it, because that was exactly what I had just had to pay for a needle and thread at the clothes shop in Bjørgvin, and now I would have to pay the same amount on Sartor, in Sund, no, this shocked me, this was absolutely unbelievable, two hundred and fifty kroner again for another needle and thread, that meant I'll have spent five hundred whole kroner on needles and thread today, and to tell the truth that was all the money I'd planned to spend on my whole trip to Bjørgvin this summer, including the cost of the fuel, which would be rather modest, no, this was unbelievable, but I'd only asked for a needle and thread, not for the price, dumb and gullible as I was, an idiot, yes, was there any bad word that didn't describe me perfectly, and now I was standing there fumbling for my wallet and there behind the counter, by the cash register, stood The Shopkeeper, all-powerful, so the only thing I could do was pay and look happy about it, as they say, I thought and I took out two hundred-kroner notes and a fifty and I'd be damned if I handed the notes to The Shopkeeper, I'd just put them down on the counter so that The Shopkeeper, greedy as she was, would have to reach out and take her money, yes, she'd actually have to show with her body how greedy she was, I thought and the second I thought that thought and put the money down on the counter the money was gone and I heard The Shopkeeper ask if there was anything else I wanted and I'd be damned if there was, even though I'd been planning to buy this and that, but if this was how it was going to be then forget it, I thought and picked up the spool of black thread and the needle, and The Shopkeeper had stuck it through a scrap of paper, she was considerate enough to do that anyway, I thought, so then, nothing else, The Shopkeeper said and I just shook my head and I was already heading for the door and I heard The Shopkeeper behind me say thanks for coming in, and then say I hope you like your needle and thread, yes, I'm sure you will, I heard her say, and her voice was a little mocking, wasn't it, I thought in the doorway as I opened the door and left and the door slid shut behind me and I thought that now I was really not in the mood to go to The Tearoom, the only thing I wanted to do was get back on board Eline and lie down on the berth and try to forget all about needles and thread and think about something else, and if I could get to sleep, yes, there'd be nothing better than that, but it'd probably take some time before I could, I thought and I lay down on the berth and tried to stretch out to my full length, I spread the blanket over me and I thought that well I wouldn't be having any dinner today, and I wasn't too hungry so that was okay, but it didn't feel nice lying there on the berth, it almost felt like something I didn't want to be doing, and I twisted and turned and I felt restlessness tingling in my body, and I also felt dammit, there was no one you could trust in the whole world, all my life I'd been stupid enough to go around thinking you could trust country people, unlike city people, or unlike Bjørgvin people in any case, Bjørgvin people always had a reputation of cheating everybody, especially anyone who was or might be from Strileland, but it wasn't true, Strileland people were no better, today I'd seen it for myself, and the swindle I'd just suffered, because it was a real swindle, pure and simple, had practically turned my worldview upside down, and anyway this word, worldview, what kind of view is that, and did I even have one, a view of what exactly, from where, no, if I didn't even know what a worldview was I probably didn't have one, because how could I, no, you tell me, and it didn't matter, what mattered was that I'd thrown away five hundred whole kroner today on two probably basically identical needles and two basically identical spools of black thread, or strictly speaking one and a half, since the one I bought from the lady in Bjørgvin had already been partly used up, maybe there was less than half the thread left for all I knew, I'd take a look tomorrow, right now I was too tired to compare how much black thread there was on the two spools, now I didn't want to think about needles or thread anymore, now I wanted to get to sleep, and luckily I never had trouble falling asleep, I'd been a sound sleeper my whole life, it was something I was blessed with, and now that was quite a phrase too, sound sleeper, sound sleeper, what does sound have to do with it, I thought and then I turned over onto my side, shut my eyes, and like I always did before I went to sleep I said the Our Father quietly to myself, even though I wasn't a believer, or I just believed in God a little, maybe, I was in the habit of saying the Our Father before I went to sleep and as I listened to the sound of the water splashing so peacefully against the hull of the boat I prayed my Our Father and the water splashed and splashed and then I suddenly woke up, because someone was saying Jatgeir, Jatgeir, I heard Jatgeir Jatgeir, and was I hearing things or was there really someone saying my name, or more like almost shouting it, but it was probably just something I'd heard in my dream, I'd dreamed that someone was saying my name, because after all I'd just fallen asleep, or dreamed that someone was not exactly saying it but kind of both whispering it and shouting it, or shouting it in a whispering way, Jatgeir, Jatgeir, there it was again, and now I couldn't be dreaming it, because now I was awake and so there had to really be someone saying my name, and it was definitely a woman's voice, and plus there was something familiar about that woman's voice wasn't there, but who could it be, saying my name, and here in Sund, it had to be coming from the quay in Sund, and in the middle of the night now too, or late in the evening anyway, because even now so close to midsummer there was a little light shining in the cabin, no, this had to be something I was just imagining, I must be hearing things, or, yes, I had heard it in my mind in a dream, I thought, but then again I couldn't be sure, because maybe there really was someone who'd said my name, yes, practically called my name, no, it couldn't be, not here, not now, so that was that, there was nothing more to think about, and I must have been tired after everything I'd been through yesterday, because even though I usually got undressed before going to bed, when I was on board the boat too, now I was lying here in the berth fully clothed, and with only a blanket over me, as usual, Jatgeir, Jatgeir, there was the voice again, and now it was clearer, louder, Jatgeir, Jatgeir, it said and again this woman's voice said Jatgeir and now I was sure I wasn't dreaming, there really was someone saying my name, and so, well, if someone was calling me I probably had to go out and see who it was, anyway it sounded like the voice was coming from the quay, and of course I wanted to know who was saying my name, I was curious of course, yes, I thought and I sat up on the berth, rubbed the sleep from my eyes with the back of my hand and stood up as straight as I could in the cabin, Jatgeir, Jatgeir the voice said again and I opened the door and left the wheelhouse and stood up straight to my full height, and I was tall, so when I was standing up straight I was hardly a little kid, no, I was a sturdy man, and then I went out on deck and I looked up at the quay and there, there on the quay, yes, there was, yes, I couldn't believe my eyes, because there she was, Eline Eline! Eline, yes, my old secret love was standing there, standing not far from the edge of the quay and looking straight at the boat I had named precisely Eline, not really knowing what I was doing, but that's what I'd done, and I'd heard that Eline was moving to somewhere on Sartor to live, but now, no, now I could see perfectly clearly, because that was my old secret love standing there, wasn't it, looking down at the boat with the name Eline proudly displayed on both sides of the cabin, now Eline was standing there, because she really was, she who had given the boat its name without knowing it, because I'd never, of course, I'd never said anything to Eline about my love for her, never, never in my life would I have dared to say something like that to a woman, no, I wasn't that kind of person, not me, no, and for Eline to be standing there now, glowing, just a few feet away from me on this beautiful summer night, no, this wasn't real, this was a dream, I was seeing things, it was a mirage, it must be, because that couldn't be Eline standing a little way back from the edge of the quay saying my name, no, it just wasn't possible, and I stared at her as she stood there and again she said Jatgeir, Jatgeir and I couldn't do anything but trust my own eyes and ears, because if I didn't do that then I was living in a dream anyway, not living on earth and Jatgeir, Jatgeir she said again and there was a kind of sad summoning in her voice, yes, almost like she was calling sheep to come back in the evening, like *seesssoo seesssoo*, Jatgeir Jatgeir like that, and now I had to answer something, the very least I had to do was give some kind of answer, yes, I thought

Yes, I said loudly

and it got quiet, and I saw Eline there on the quay taking a step or two back, wasn't she, and my voice had maybe been a bit abrupt, saying yes like that, yes, well, but I couldn't believe it, that it was Eline who had said my name and who was now kind of half darting back along the quay, no it was unbelievable, and since I wasn't dreaming now I had to be seeing things pure and simple because I thought I'd heard at The Vaim General Store that Eline had got married to a man from Sartor, yes, that's what they were saying, yes, someone had asked if she'd got engaged, and they'd said that the man she'd got engaged to was a real Sartor Strileland guy, a fisherman by trade, they'd said, but no one had said anything about where on Sartor he was from, or maybe I could vaguely remember that someone had said something about Sund, yes, maybe, maybe someone had told me that Eline had moved to Sund, or maybe I just overheard it at The Vaim General Store or maybe this thing about Eline and Sund was just something I'd imagined, but there, right there on the quay, not twenty feet away from me, there, I now saw, Eline had stopped and she stood there facing me, mirage or not, seeing things or not, the fact was Eline was standing there on the quay and looking right at me, and if I was seeing things then I was seeing them as truly as anyone can possibly see anything, yes, so it was really like there was something you could see and I was just seeing it, and I stood there, on Eline's deck, looking at the Eline I'd named my boat after, without her knowing it, at least I hoped she didn't know it, but anyway we couldn't just stay standing like that, because now we'd been standing like that for a long time, yes, it felt like we'd been standing like that for a very long time, and since she, Eline, had spoken first, had said my name, it was probably my turn now to say something, and since Eline had said my name loud and clear, it was probably my turn now to say her name loud and clear and I sort of gathered up my strength and then I said Eline loud and clear and I couldn't help it, there was something like a trembling love in my voice, or something like longing, more than anything it was like I'd said the name Eline in a pleading voice, and I didn't mean to, not at all, it just came out like that, I couldn't help it, so much longing, so many years of longing, had I guess built up in me that I couldn't keep it inside, it entered into the name Eline when I said it just now, and after all I'd said the name Eline to myself so many times, but hardly ever said it to anyone else, and anyway never to her herself, to Eline in person, but now I'd done it, for the first time, and it was like the name Eline was hanging in the air, as they say, and it hung there for a long time, an endless long time, it felt like, and then Eline said in a loud but teary voice

Yes, she said

and that yes kind of sank into me, yes, it was almost like I swallowed the word and it got stuck in my stomach, and the yes was like the answer to a huge question, and it was not like any ordinary yes, it was more like the kind of yes I imagined someone would say when they were asked if they wanted to marry the person standing there next to them, it was that kind of yes, and once again I didn't know what to say and I looked down and then I peeked up and I saw Eline standing there on the quay looking down at the ground in front of her, and now I needed to say something out loud, but what should I say, in this strange and wonderful moment, this moment I'd been longing for and dreaming of for a year and a day, probably all the way back into my younger years, not to say my youth, but still, well, all right I admit it, it did sometimes happen that I dreamed of Eline and longed for her and said her name to myself, it did happen, but not that often, and sometimes, to tell the truth, I wasn't sure if I was thinking about my boat when I was standing on its deck or if I was thinking about Eline who was now standing here large as life in the half-dark summer night, here on the quay in Sund, and then I heard Eline say Jatgeir again, and she said my name with longing in her voice, and then I see her walk down to the edge of the quay towards my boat, towards me, but now I really must be dreaming, because this can't be real, I think, but it probably must be real, I think and I rub my eyes with the backs of my hands and I pinch my arm, yes, by god I pinch myself on the arm, and I'm awake, wide awake, and Eline is coming down to the edge of the quay, and I probably have to do something, say something, I probably can't just stay standing here looking at her feet, which are now all I can see of her, yes, she's come so close to the boat and I don't really know what to say to Eline, but most likely she'll say something first, since she's the one who's come to me and not me to her, so it's probably up to her to talk first, I think and then I stand there on the deck and I don't even dare to look up at Eline, and she doesn't say anything, so I guess I do need to say something

Hello, I say

Hello, Eline says

and then neither of us says anything

It's been a long time, I say

Yes, a year and a day, she says

and again neither of us says anything and I pull myself together

It's wonderful to see you again, I say

Thank you, same here, she says

and again neither of us says anything and I think now someone needs to say something

No, it's certainly a surprise, I say

Yes, seeing you again like this, and here in Sund, I say

No, I never would have believed this could happen, I say

Never in the world, she says

and she says that like she's trying to be on the safe side, I think and again neither of us says anything and I think again that I've got to say something, but I probably can't ask Eline to come on board the boat now, at night, a married woman and everything

Can I come on board, Eline says

Yes, of course, please do, I say

Please do, I repeat

and I see that Eline, who knows her way around a boat, is already climbing down from the quay, and then there she is in person standing right there on the gunwale, Eline, I think and I smile at the thought that, yes, now Eline is standing on Eline, I think and it's like Eline can read my mind because she says

Yes, now Eline is standing on Eline, she says

and I think how could Eline know that the boat is

called Eline, and then I think what a stupid thought that is, because Eline is written right there on the side of the cabin in big letters, she'd have to be almost blind not to see that even in the half-darkness, I think

So you named your boat Eline, did you, Eline says

and she's still standing on the gunwale

I did, yes, I say

and I think that it probably makes sense to hold out my hand to help Eline on board, and I hold out my hand and Eline grabs my hand with such feeling, so warmly, and it's like the warmth from her hand runs through my whole body, in a way I've never felt before either, this warm feeling through my whole body was new to me, I think, and it's a feeling I can't name, it can't be said in words, I think as I stand there holding Eline's hand even though she's now standing firmly on the deck safe and sound, and she, Eline, holds my hand tight and clearly doesn't want to let it go, and if she doesn't want to let go of my hand then I certainly don't want to let go of her hand, I think and so we just stand there, hand in hand, on the deck, and my goodness I can't even count how many times I've dreamed of holding Eline's hand, I think, and now in the half-darkness, in the half-light, on a midsummer's night, off the quay in Sund, on my boat Eline, there we stand now, hand in hand, hand in hand at last, I think, but we can't do something like this, because Eline is a married woman, it's been many years since she left Vaim, pretty suddenly, and moved away, and not long after that, I don't remember exactly when it was, people said she was going to get married to a guy from Sartor, and there were probably also whispers from here and there that she had to get married, that she was already pregnant, but people say so many things, you should never assume rumours are true, I thought, and we can't just stay standing like this, one of

us has to say something, I thought
   Yes, here you are at last, Eline says then
   Yes, I say
   It took us many years to find each other, she says
   and I thought the same thing and felt the same thing but to say it out loud, no, that was too much, I couldn't do that, not before and not now, and I stayed standing there looking down, and I couldn't stay standing like that, we couldn't stay standing like that, I thought and I looked up and I saw Eline standing there next to me, just standing up straight in the half-dark midsummer's night, and she hadn't changed a bit, she was exactly the same after all these years, no, it's unbelievable, I must be dreaming, this isn't real, I think and Eline says that it's unbelievable we've met again now, and how could I even know she lived in Sund, no she shouldn't have said that, now why did she say that, she says and I think why is Eline saying that now, that it's unbelievable I knew she lived in Sund, because of course I didn't know that, so why is she asking about that, I think and Eline says that I must have heard talk back home in Vaim and again Eline says now why did she say that and I say that I probably need to invite her in, she should come in, yes, if I can't invite her into my house then I should at least invite her into my boat's cabin, I don't have any other place I can invite her into, I say and Eline says thank you and then she goes into the cabin and I think that now I don't understand what's going on, I don't understand anything, now I can't be awake, because this must be a dream, and it's not like it matters much, a dream is a dream and reality is reality, but in a way reality has probably always been, yes, no, no not like a dream, but reality has had something dreamlike about it too probably my whole life, reality is in the dream the way the boat is in the water, I think, or maybe the other way

around, the water is the reality and the boat is the dream, because a boat is probably always a dream of something or another, yes, definitely, that's what a boat is for sure and certain, that's what it was for me anyway, I don't know exactly what dream but the boat had always been some kind of dream, ever since I was a little boy, I think and I hear Eline say from the cabin aren't I coming in with her soon and I go in and I see that Eline has sat down on my sheets and not on the empty berth on the port side, and now where should I sit, I can't sit next to Eline, I don't think, but, there would somehow also be something wrong about sitting on the other bench, the free bench, which I never use as a berth anyway, while Eline is sitting over there on what you'd have to call if not my bed, since there aren't beds on a boat, then my berth anyway, I think and I hear Eline say I should sit down too, and so I sit right smack down on the berth next to Eline, and neither of us says anything, and so we sit there looking straight ahead and I think someone has to say something and then I say that it sure was nice to see you again after all these years, I say and Eline says that yes, yes it really was, and then there's silence and I think that I need to ask Eline how she knew that this was my motorboat, and how she knew I was on board, I think and then I hear Eline say that she was in The Grocery Store today for a minute and she caught a glimpse of me and then I went on board the boat and then she went home, yes, home, well, just because you call a place home doesn't mean it's a home, and at home she couldn't get me out of her mind, yes, it was just like back in the old days, she said, and she stopped, and my goodness she blushed a little, sitting there, even in the half-dark cabin I could, not see it, no, but I could kind of tell, and then there was silence

So you ended up on Sartor, I say then

I did, yes, Eline says
Here in Sund, she says
You got married here, I say
Married, she says
and then neither of us says anything and I think that someone has to say something
Because you're married right, I say
Yes, well, she says
Unfortunately, unfortunately I got married here, but I never really found my place here, she says
and then neither of us says anything, for a long time
I want to go to Vaim with you, Eline says
and I can't believe it, what is she saying, go to Vaim with me, she gets on board my boat late in the evening, at night, and then says she wants to go to Vaim with me, no, this, this, I think
Yes, home to Vaim, Eline says
and I often don't know what to say but now I really don't know what to say
But aren't you married to someone from Sartor, don't you live here in Sund, I say
and Eline says she is, but it isn't a happy marriage, she says and she starts crying, she should never have married that man, Frank, she says in tears, that was the dumbest thing she ever did in her life, she did it right after she left Vaim, moved away, to Bjørgvin, she says, but now she wants to go home, she says and I ask doesn't she have children and she says that she luckily never got pregnant, at least that didn't happen, she would have loved to have a child but not with him, with Frank, as the father, she says, and can't she, can't she just get a ride in my boat back to Vaim, she says, can't I help her get away from Frank, she says, yes, she says, her bags are already packed, yes, no one's at home, her husband, Frank, he's a fisherman

and he's out at sea now so if you look at it that way there couldn't be a better time, she says, and you and me, we've always, and now she really gets red, yes we've always liked each other, and I get totally embarrassed as I sit there, no I shouldn't have said that, she says, now she's all embarrassed, she says and I just sit there and I don't know what I should say, but if you don't want me to, Eline says and she stands up

    Are you leaving, I say

    I can if you want, she says

    No, wait, I say

    Do you really want me to stay, she says

    Yes of course, I say

    and it feels like I better say it

    I've missed you all these years, always, I say

    and at the same time I think no I can't say that, I can think it, yes, but say it, no, that's not who I am, I'm not myself anymore, I can't possibly do something like that, I think and at the same time, before I know it, Eline is sitting in my lap and she puts her arm around my shoulder and she kisses me on the cheek and she says can't we leave right now and I ask her doesn't she want to bring anything with her and she says with a short sharp laugh that she's already packed, she packed the things she wants in a suitcase and she hid it behind some bushes at the bend in the road, yes just before the road gets down to the quay, at first she thought she'd bring the suitcase with her right away, but then she started thinking that it would be too presumptuous, since after all it wasn't even a sure thing that I was planning to go straight home to Vaim, and if I wasn't planning to leave for home right away then it also wasn't a sure thing that I'd want her as a passenger, or a stowaway I guess, she said, but now that she was going to come home to Vaim with me she would go and get her suitcase, if that's okay with me, she says, she'd go and get her suitcase right now and I probably don't answer fast enough because she says that well I probably don't want her to come with me and I sort of wake up and I see her standing in the cabin door and without exactly knowing what I'm doing I stand up and go over to her and put my arms around her and she puts her arms around me and then we stand there hugging each other and stand there for, no, I don't know how long, but then she whispers in my ear that now she should probably go and get her suitcase and I say yes, I say it in a shaky voice, and we let go of each other and then Eline steps up onto the gunwale as easy as can be and up across the floating deck hanging off the side of the quay and then she disappears into the half-darkness and I think what just happened, I don't understand anything, it's true I'd liked Eline all these years but I never said anything to her about it, not one single word, and I never did anything that could have implied it, and now it seems like she must have known it somehow, and she must have maybe, yes, definitely, liked me too, no, this, miracle of miracles, no, this, no, I couldn't understand it, it was what they call incomprehensible, inconceivable, unbelievable, I thought and then I sat down on the berth where Eline had just been sitting and I thought I should have cleaned the boat and tidied up, but of course I wasn't expecting a visit, and if Eline was thinking of coming with me all the way home, to my house, yes, that would be great, but I hadn't cleaned house for a long time, and tidied up, no I couldn't remember the last time I'd tidied up the place, but anyway who said Eline wanted to come home with me, no one, no, absolutely no one, that was just something I got carried away and thought of, it, I just imagined it, it's nothing but wishful thinking, and maybe the whole thing was my imagination, yes, that

Eline had been on my boat, yes, maybe it was something I had in a way dreamed, yes, that must be what had happened, it couldn't actually be true that Eline had been on my boat and said she wanted to come home to Vaim with me, she hadn't said anything about where she was going to live there either, but she'd probably never thought about moving in with me, and did I want that, really, wouldn't I much rather keep living alone, the way I'd done, yes, since my parents died, and that was getting to be some years ago now, but now there was kind of no discussion of what I wanted or didn't want, now it was like someone else's will was making the decisions, everything had kind of changed all at once, now it was kind of Eline's will that was deciding everything, no, this wasn't something I should think any more about, now it was going to happen however it was going to happen, however it had to happen, because now it was probably already decided that Eline would come home to Vaim with me, she had just now gone to get her suitcase, and that was no dream, it was certain reality, for better or worse, yes, it felt like my future was decided now, everything was different now, and there was nothing I could do but go along with what had happened as best as I could, but everything felt so unreal, yes, like it couldn't be anything but a dream, but it wasn't a dream, I was standing right here as wide awake as can be on the deck in the cabin of the motorboat Eline, I was even standing with my legs apart, and it was as sure and certain as anything could be that Eline had been here, on board, and now she'd gone to get her suitcase that she'd left behind some bushes up by the bend in the road, and hadn't we even stood here and hugged each other, yes, we had, there was no denying it, and wasn't that just before we'd kissed each other? or maybe not? but had I really tried to kiss her, no I would never try to kiss her, so I don't understand why I thought that, but a thought is a thought, and hadn't I often, so so often, thought about wanting to kiss Eline, and more than that, yes the truth is I had, and not just once or twice either, if I'm being honest, yes, I was crazy about Eline back then, and my being crazy about her never entirely stopped even though I knew perfectly well that Eline had moved to Sartor and had found a good husband there, yes, even though I knew that I hadn't stopped being crazy about her, if anything the feeling had got even stronger, and that's why, maybe that's exactly why I had moored for the night in Sund too, even though I hadn't thought it was because of Eline, but even if someone doesn't think something, yes, they can still do something or another, a person can moor his boat in Sund and there must be some reason or another he does that, because I could just as well have gone somewhere else in my boat, or stayed in Bjørgvin, no, I couldn't bear to do that and that was because of those damn buttons, but how could I think of those loose buttons at a time like this, didn't I have other things to think about now besides needles and thread, yes, I certainly did, but damn, being ripped off twice on the same day, and by both a Bjørgvin person and a Strileland person, or a city lady and a country lady I should probably say, or however you'd put it, I'd been ripped off, shamefully ripped off, both back there in Bjørgvin and out here on Sartor, and to be cheated by a Strileland person too, no, I wouldn't have expected that, I'd thought Strileland people were better than Bjørgvin people, but I'd sure been wrong about that, embarrassingly wrong, there was nothing else to say about that, and now, when Eline comes back should I tell her about it? about how much money I was cheated out of today, and just because a button or two had come loose and I was in Bjørgvin because I needed to buy a needle and thread, in recent years it'd just been one trip a year I took to Bjørgvin, not like when I was young, no, back then I would always be taking the motorboat to Bjørgvin, in the summer anyway, starting in the spring, but it was different now, especially since my parents had passed, but maybe mostly because I'd got older and I didn't enjoy going out to bars and restaurants anymore, because, yes, when I was younger I was probably really out looking for women, as they say, or I simply wanted to find a wife, like other men, not to say an old lady, the way guys tend to call them, but out in the country I didn't meet anyone, or however you'd say it, probably there was something in me, a shyness, that made me never really try, or put myself forward, or however you'd put it, yes, I never approached a woman in any way, and no woman ever so much as looked at me, not that I was ugly or anything, I probably looked like any ordinary guy, nothing was wrong with me, maybe my beard was a bit bigger and longer than most men's, yes, that's true, I had a big full beard, and when I felt like it had got too long, yes, I'd stand in front of the bathroom mirror and trim it with scissors, but to tell the truth a long time could go by between times I brought out the scissors, that's how it was, but I tended to always trim my beard whenever I took my boat to Bjørgvin, and I'd usually also cut my hair then too, and my hairstyle, if that's what you call it, was nice and simple, I'd always brush my hair back and then cut it along the back of my neck as best I could, first straight across, and then I'd try to cut a little more first on one side and then on the other, someone who lived alone had to manage as best he could, because I couldn't just go down into town and ask if someone wanted to cut my hair, or maybe ask if someone could just stand behind me and tell me how to cut it, no, so the easiest and best thing to do was just do it myself even if it sometimes ended up shorter on one side than the other, that's just how it had to be, it didn't matter that much, it didn't look bad at all from the front and that was the most important thing, it didn't matter as much how I looked from the back, that's what I did for all those years, that's how it was, my beard and hair had been black my whole life but in recent years more and more grey had spread through it, both my hair and my beard, and now it was probably half grey, and there are probably some women who don't care about that, that's what they say, so yes, there I was, a half-grey middle-aged man, and I could understand that perfectly well, and so then and there I gave up for good on finding a woman, there's that way of talking again, finding a woman, but I'd never been able to stop thinking about Eline, and now, now I was standing in the middle of the deck of my boat, Eline, in the cabin, wasn't I, and waiting for Eline to come back, and with her suitcase too, yes, probably a whole mountain of stuff, and Eline wanted to come home to Vaim, she'd said, but where was she going to live, her parents were long since dead of course and her childhood home by the bend in the road right before you got to The General Store had been sold, and as far as I knew Eline didn't have any relatives in Vaim, so what was she thinking she'd do, where would she live, no, I didn't know, for all I knew she was thinking she'd live with me, but strictly speaking did I really want someone else living in my house, bachelor that I was, in the house I'd been in my whole life, I actually didn't want anyone else living in my house, someone who pretty certainly would start by straightening everything up, yes, that was probably the word she'd use, yes, straightening up my mess, is what she'd probably say, straightening, mess, it was probably going to be a huge fuss and commotion, and even if I liked Eline so much, no, I don't know, most likely I'm just too old now anyway to want to adapt to living with someone else, no, what a fine mess I've got myself into now, because the cold hard truth is that Eline has just gone to get her suitcase and there's nothing I can do but stand here waiting for her to get back, and there, yes, I hear footsteps there and I step up onto the gunwale and hold the edge of the quay and there she is, I see Eline coming taking big strides and carrying a huge suitcase, so this is more real than maybe I entirely realized, until I saw Eline coming straight towards me now and she's walking so fast that the suitcase is swinging back and forth as she walks, and I've probably never seen a bigger suitcase in my life, yes, you could probably call that an American suitcase, I think, but a suitcase like that, an American suitcase, yes, is probably more like a chest but how can I just stand here and think about how an American suitcase looks, of all things, while Eline is coming at full speed towards me, yes, she's walking so fast that she's almost running, she must be in a real hurry to get on board with me, no this is more than I could have imagined, I think and Eline has got to the edge of the quay and she hands me the suitcase and it's not as heavy as it looked, and it's no problem to take the suitcase and lift it on board and put it down on the deck, and I turn around and I see that Eline is already climbing on board, she is already standing on the gunwale and holding onto the handrail on the cabin, and then she comes on board, and once she's on board she asks when I was thinking of heading north and I hadn't really thought about it in detail but I probably wasn't planning to stay moored at the quay in Sund past tomorrow in any case

Tomorrow, I say

But, Eline says

Can't we go a bit north and find some place to cast

anchor up there, she says

and I think what kind of an idea is that, now, so late at night or in the early hours of the morning or whatever time it is, and besides I don't have sheets on board for more than one person, but now it seems like Eline will be sleeping on board too, how can she think we should leave now, I think

Please, Eline says

and I don't really understand why Eline is saying this to me in such a pleading voice, but if she feels that strongly about it and asks like it's so important then I can't really do anything except what she asks, she just wants to get away from Sund, she wants to escape in spite of everything and running away, as far away as possible, seems to be the only thing in her head, I think and I can understand that, she's leaving her husband and child, no she doesn't have a child, and that's good at least, it's probably better that she doesn't, yes, imagine having a screaming kid or two on board as well, but luckily it was just Eline, as if that wasn't enough, no, how can I think such a thing, when all my life I've been, yes, dreaming about Eline, hung up on Eline, you could honestly say that she'd been the only woman in my life, not that she was really in my life, of course, but in my mind she was the only woman in my life, there was no one else, and for all I know maybe it was for the best like that, for it to stay like that, because it was something very different once she was really here, like now in my boat, I think and I hear Eline say can't we leave soon and I think now why does she want that really, isn't she tired, is it just me who's tired, because I'd just got to sleep, and leaving now, no, I don't really want to do that, although the current was good, and I've always been interested in maps, sea charts, so I could read them as well as anyone, at least for the waterways where I usually went with my boat, and I can steer in the dark by the navigation lights in the water, yes, I can do that, I can manage to do that, I've done it lots of times, but I wouldn't exactly say I like steering the boat in the dark, or in the half-dark, when I was younger I sometimes liked doing that but not anymore, and I'm tired and I want to sleep

    You need to leave tonight, Eline says

    Okay, I say

    You have to, she says

    and it's like she's almost begging me

    Okay, I say again

    Actually right now, she says

    and I don't answer, what's the damn hurry, I think

    It's important, Eline says

    Okay, I say

    Because he might come home any minute, yes, she says

    He, I say

    Yes, she says

    and there's silence

    He's a fisherman, you know, she says

    And I never know for sure when he's coming back home, she says

    He could come home any minute, she says

    And they often tie up here, yes, right here where you tied up, she says

    They're coming home some time tonight anyway, she says

    Okay, I say

    Yes, Eline says

    So let's go right now, she says

    He works with two other fishermen on a ship, she says

    And the ship is called Elinor, she says

    But now he's decided he wants to start fishing alone and he's bought himself a boat, it's supposed to get delivered tomorrow, she says

But can we afford it, she says

No of course not, she says

And then he'll have to buy everything else he needs, all kinds of fishing equipment, no, that never goes well, she says

We won't be able to put food on the table, she says

But he wants his own big boat he can fish on alone, a sjark, that's what he wants, she says

and I don't know what to say and then I hear Eline say we need to hurry, they might come any minute, and without thinking about it any more I turn the key and start the motor and it starts right up as always and gives a nice little purr the way it always does, yes, it's an excellent motor, nothing's ever gone wrong with it, not one single time, and how many years have I had this boat and this motor by now, it's been quite a few years, yes, I think and I hear Eline say that she's so worried that the ship, and he, could come around that headland there, and she points out to sea in the half-dark and I think that now it probably won't be long until the night is at its darkest, if it isn't already, because on summer nights like this it never really gets fully dark, and so strictly speaking I don't need to navigate that much differently than I do during the day, I think and I hear Eline ask if she should untie the mooring lines and I say she can just go into the cabin, I can untie them myself, and she says that she can do it too and she's already heading up to the edge of the quay, she's really fast, I think and now she's untied the stern line, and thrown the rope on deck, and Eline is standing back on deck in front of me, legs apart, coiling the rope, yes, she knows her way around a boat and she's quick too, Eline is, I think and the boat has already drifted a good ways out from the quay, so now I just need to wait until Eline is

safely back in the wheelhouse and then I'll turn the boat
and set a course north, I think, because Eline will probably remember to take in the fenders too, and I see Eline
standing and coiling up the line I'd moored the stern of
the boat with and now the Eline slides slowly away from
the quay and I see Eline walk on the gunwale to the front
deck and she loosens the fenders at the bow and then
walks back down the gunwale with them, as I thought,
Eline brought the fenders on board, yes, she's been in a
boat before, I think, she's a hard-working woman, and I
give the boat a little gas and now my beautiful motorboat
Eline is gliding slowly forwards on the dead calm water
and I stand at the helm and I think I'll wait a minute
before sitting down in the captain's chair, I don't know
why but I feel like waiting for whatever reason and now
Eline will probably bring the stern fenders on board too,
I think and I think about how many times I've sat in this
chair while the Eline glides quietly and peacefully along
the shore, I think and I glance back and there I see Eline
looking back towards land and I think that she's standing there now looking back, looking at the life she's left,
at the house where she lived, lived for many years now,
how many, no I don't know, but it must have been a lot,
because she was just a girl when she moved away from
Vaim, back when I was so, yes, well, what can I say, yes, I
was so – no, in love is the wrong word, it's like I'm not one
of the people who use words like that, but yes, yes, I was
hung up on her, yes, I can say that much, I can accept that
much, I think and I turn around again and Eline is still
standing there looking at the shore and obviously she's
looking at the house where she lived for so many years,
a house she'll now most likely never see again, and even
if she wants to leave her home it must probably still feel
sad and strange to leave like this, run away from home

in a way, but there, around the headland there, a ship is coming and its course is headed straight towards us, it's coming pretty fast and I turn hard to starboard and I hear Eline say as she slips into the cabin that that was a close call, if she hadn't realized she had to get us to cast off then they could really have been in trouble, yes, and now she has to hide, she says standing in the door to the cabin, so that no one on board the Elinor sees her, because it's there, on that boat, that her husband, yes, her husband is, she says from the door to the cabin and she looks at me

He mustn't see me, no one on the ship can see me, she says

and I don't say anything and she says that now the ship, Elinor, is about to reach land and so all three of the men on board are probably up in the wheelhouse, and the ship with Elinor in big letters on the front of the wheelhouse gets closer and I see three heads there and they're looking out the wheelhouse window

There are three men there looking out, I say

and Eline doesn't say anything

And now we're passing right by each other, I say

and I see that Eline isn't standing in the door to the cabin anymore and she's probably sat down on one of the benches there, I think and just as we pass each other with only forty or fifty feet between us I raise my hand and wave and the man standing at Elinor's helm raises his hand and waves, the way people do on the water, and damn if he doesn't raise his sailor's cap a little off his head and I turn hard to starboard so that the wake from the ship doesn't hit the side of the boat, the ship is travelling at a good speed and leaving more of a wake than you'd think a ship like that could leave, I think, and now the bow of the Eline rocks up and down, no, I was crazy enough to name my boat Eline, and since the name is on both sides of the wheelhouse the men on the Elinor must have seen the name, no, that's embarrassing, I think, it's almost enough to make me turn red, I think, no, how could I ever have come up with the idea of doing that, and it was before Eline moved away from Vaim too, that's when I bought this boat, and then, back in those days, well, I must not have been thinking too clearly when I named it after Eline, and it probably never occurred to me that Eline might one day see the boat and the name on the boat with her own eyes, no, and then that she'd not just see the boat but come on board it, no, this, I think and I hear Eline say that the ship must be at the quay now and I turn around and I see that the ship is floating backward towards the quay, and it looks to me like it's mooring exactly where the Eline had been, so it was definitely a good idea of Eline's to get me to leave, I think and I hear Eline say damn it's a good thing she thought of that, yes, it's good that she could get away from Sund and from all of Sartor and back home to Vaim just by packing the suitcase and coming on board my boat, she says, but it seems like she hadn't had much time, she'd probably had a feeling that the Elinor was on its way home, and that was probably why she'd packed in such a hurry, yes, she hadn't been able to bring that much with her, just the most necessary things, and the ones that meant the most to her, like a picture of her parents in front of their house in Vaim, in front of the house where she grew up, and she'd had a good childhood, the only thing was it was too bad she'd been such a silly girl and not known what was best for her and had left home as soon as she could, and for nothing except to toil away as a maid for a rich Bjørgvin family flush with old money, so she was certainly beside herself with joy when Frank proposed to her on the third night after they'd met, and she said yes, and then she was living in his house on Sartor, the house there in Sund, the house he'd inherited from his parents, they were well along in years when he was born, Frank, yes, and they, his parents, yes, they were long since dead when she met him so he had lived alone there in his childhood home for many years, and that's what it looked like too, because no one had straightened up or cleaned the place since, yes, it must have been since his mother died, and that was quite a few years back by then, and not many people had walked through the door of that house after his parents passed, first his father passed, and a couple of years later his mother, but that was an incredibly long time ago now, yes, he'd lived alone for years and years before he got a wife, as they say, got himself a wife, she says and she sighs, yes, he got himself a woman, yes, but now he didn't have a woman anymore, she wished she could see his face when he got home and didn't find her anywhere, first he'd look in the bedroom, and then he'd shout for her, Eline he'd shout, and then he'd walk through the whole house looking for her, but she wouldn't be anywhere, and then he'd eventually see the quick letter she'd written him and left on the kitchen table, where she wrote that she'd had enough, she'd left now, moved out, and she didn't need anything she couldn't take with her in a single suitcase, he could just keep it all, his things and her things, everything in the house, she didn't want any of it, and then she wrote, she said, that she wanted to thank him for their time together, it was what it was, but now it was time to end it, so thanks for everything, she'd written, and she didn't blame him for anything and wasn't mad about anything, but she didn't say the opposite either, and she hadn't written a word about where she was going, but he probably wasn't so dumb that he wouldn't realize it himself, because she'd talked about Vaim so many times and about how she wanted to go back there, she'd been homesick, she said, and he, Frank, had always said that he could understand that, during the years he was away from Sund, yes, when he was in the military, he'd been homesick a lot, he had probably never appreciated Sund and all of Sartor, yes, even Bjørgvin, as much as during the years he was a soldier in the far north, in Finnmark, back when he was walking around here like he did every day it was like he didn't see it, didn't see how nice it was in Sund, or on the whole island of Sartor, or in Bjørgvin either for that matter, nothing he saw up in Finnmark could compare to what there was to see on Sartor, and especially you could look at the ocean here on Sartor, see the sun go down behind the sea, or see it come up out of the sea, yes, that's what he'd said, things like that, and then she'd say again how much she missed home and then he wouldn't say anything more, he never said a word about them maybe going to Vaim someday, even just taking a trip there, no, it was like Vaim didn't exist for him, like there wasn't anywhere in the world called Vaim, like Vaim was just a dreamworld, but both of them, yes, both she and Jatgeir knew that Vaim was a very real place, they had both grown up in Vaim, so for both of them the town of Vaim was one of the realest places in the world, even if you had to wonder just then at the moment what was real and what wasn't, unreal as she was, yes, I couldn't understand a thing, no, it was simply unbelievable actually that she, Eline, was now standing in the door to the cabin talking to me, yes, just chatting away while we headed away from Sund, from Sartor, from her old life, or maybe more like her interim life, or however you'd say that, she said, anyway she was now heading off to a new life in Vaim, she said, to a new life in the Vaim of her childhood, in the Vaim of her childhood that was now going to be the Vaim of her years as a mature woman too, she said and then she pointed and said look there's Bjørgvin and I had already seen for a while that we were putting Bjørgvin behind us now, and there behind us, on this side of the fjord, there was Sartor and far behind us now was Sund, but we couldn't see anything in this half-dark summer night, maybe just a vague shape, and it was good to put both Bjørgvin and Sund and all of Sartor behind me, because it hadn't been a good day, I'd been thoroughly ripped off both in Bjørgvin and in Sund, there was no other way to put it, I just wanted to do something as simple as buy myself a needle and a spool of black thread to sew a loose button or two back on, a needle and thread shouldn't cost that much, I'd thought, but since they didn't seem to have anything like that at The Vaim General Store I'd just buy it somewhere else, but I didn't think they would have anything like that for sale at The Grocery Store in Sund, no, and if they had it there they could very well have it at The Vaim General Store too, but I couldn't know that, because I'd never asked if they had needle and thread there, I had taken it for granted that they didn't sell things like that there, but for all I knew they actually did have both needles and thread at The Vaim General Store and for a low price too, no, I hadn't ever thought of that, and now it would be almost worse if they did have it, so I would never ask for needle and thread at The Vaim General Store, I think and Eline says that I seem lost in thought and I think can I really tell Eline now about how I'd been cheated twice today, or yesterday you'd probably have to say by this point, yes, thoroughly cheated, robbed of my money twice when I was buying a needle and thread since some of my buttons had come loose and needed to be sewn back on, no, I had to stop thinking about that, even if that, I thought

What are you thinking about, Eline asks
Nothing, I say
No, okay, she says
and neither of us says anything
You don't want to say, she says
But I'm so curious, she says
Please tell me, she says
and she gives me a little poke in the side
I'm thinking about a needle and thread, I say
About a needle and thread, she says
and she looks like she's about to start laughing
What colour thread, she says
Black, I say
And the needle, is it a big one or a small one, short or long, I mean, she says
Just medium, I say
To sew buttons on with, she says
Yes, I say
Did you buy that today, she says
Yes, I say
and I think that I don't want to say any more than that, no one other than me and the people who ripped me off would ever know I was ripped off so badly, but of course the people who ripped me off could always laugh and brag about it to someone else
To sew buttons back on with, she says again
Yes, I say
You know, she says
You know, I thought that a needle and thread might come in handy and so I brought several sewing needles and spools of thread in different colours with me, to sew buttons on with, she says
Ah, I say
Yes isn't that a little odd, she says

Yeah, I say
and it's quiet
I can sew those buttons back on for you, she says
and I can't believe it, because that means she really was thinking of coming home with me, and what could she possibly be thinking, I think, no, it was clear, there was never any question of anything else, she was going to move in with me whether I wanted it or not, without even asking me if that was something I wanted, she just came to my boat, the motorboat Eline, she came up to me totally unexpectedly and now there was nothing else for me to do but let her live with me, I couldn't just drop her off at The Quay below The Vaim General Store, I think, now how could I even think that, imagine ever thinking something like that, I think and then Eline asks if we can't go all the way to Vaim tonight, she wants so much to get home, she says and I say that that's fine, it's not far, and I've taken this route lots of times so we should be there by morning, I say

Oh that'll be so nice, Eline says
Finally going home, she says
Finally going back to Vaim, she says
and there's a long silence and then Eline asks where I have my needle and spool of black thread and I feel in my jacket pocket and there they are, both spools, one needle stuck into what's left of the thread on one spool and the other needle in a bag with the other spool, and I take them out and hand them to Eline and she says I bought two needles and two spools and I say yes they come like that sometimes

But there's only a little thread left on one of these spools, she says
I know, I say

II

But there, isn't that a knock on the door, yes it definitely is, and there, there's another knock, and I can't remember anyone knocking on my door in a long time, the last person to do it was Jatgeir, but that stopped when that woman moved in with him and turned everything upside down, so it's been years now since he knocked on my door, but I guess it could be Jatgeir, and I'd probably better open the door then, but there are dirty dishes in the sink, and they've been there for several days, not that I use so many dishes, but still, there might even be a little mould, and when's the last time I aired out the place, no, not since I can remember, so it smells stuffy, yes, that's the least you could say about it, it probably smells like me too, and everything in here's just a mess, in the hall, in the kitchen, in the living room, there are books everywhere, books and newspapers piled up on top of each other, and so if there's a knock at the door and someone wants to come in here, to my mess, to my house's mess, no, if only I'd known that someone was going to knock on my door, but how could I have thought that would happen now that Jatgeir doesn't come by anymore, because it's been a year and a day since the last time he stopped by, and there's another knock, no, I can't believe it, and was the knock louder this time? maybe the knock was louder, or probably it's just that I could hear it better this time and that's why it sounded louder, yes, that must be what it was, but there's another knock, because that is knocking right? yes, it is, but weaker this time, yes, almost inaudible, maybe that was another knock or maybe it wasn't, but I probably need to go open the door either way, it may well be Jatgeir, maybe he suddenly thought he should drop by and see me, or it might be someone else, there are probably lots of reasons why someone might knock, maybe it's someone coming with an important message for me, maybe someone's died, but what relatives of mine could have died, no, I don't know, but it could be something, yes, important, because I don't have a telephone, and they probably wouldn't send news that someone had died by letter, no, I can't imagine that would ever happen, but there weren't that many knocks, so now the person knocking must have given up since I didn't open the door, and since the lights are on in the house the person who's knocking probably thought that I didn't want to open the door but there, yes, there's another knock, and I can probably just open the door, I probably don't need to invite whoever it is in, unless it's Jatgeir of course, yes, that's a strange name he has, Jatgeir, but it was his nickname, he told me that time I went to Bjørgvin with him on his motorboat that his name was Geir, he was baptized Geir, but that when he was young everyone started calling him Jatgeir, and I don't really know why, but maybe because he always said yes to things when he was little, he said ja, ja, he always went along with things, he always *jatta*, and that sounds plausible, but no one really knows why he's Jatgeir now, but he is, yes, so I need to invite him in, but only if it's him, if it isn't Jatgeir then we can probably just talk at the door, maybe, yes, why didn't I think of that before, I can just open the door and then the person knocking and I can just stand in the doorway and talk, yes, of course, and there's another knock, but this time it's not hard and not soft either, it's just a knock, just a little rap on the door, no more no less, but now, yes, now I'll go open the door, no more dawdling and thinking it over now, no, out to the hall and over to the door, straight there and right now, absolutely, so yes, I think and I open the living room door and go out into the hall and just then there's another knock, but now it's almost inaudible and that's strange since just now the knocks were clear enough, but not loud, or soft, just knocking, a rap on the door, no more no less, but now, yes, now I'll open the door, no more dawdling and thinking it over now, no, out to the hall and over to the door, straight there and right now, absolutely, so yes, I think and I go over to the front door and just then there's another knock, but now it's almost inaudible and that's strange since just now the knocks were clear enough, but anyway I need to open the door now, it's not the end of the world, it's just that it's been such a long time since anyone's knocked on my door, so now – there's another knock, and was it harder this time? or? but there, there, it's another knock anyway and now I open the door, and since I never lock the door I just need to open it, and so I push down on the handle and I open the door and I look out and I don't know who I think will be there, I have no idea, but no one's there and no, I would never have thought that, that no one would be there, because how was there a knocking all by itself, there's no one in sight, no, this is almost spooky, but the person knocking can't just have left right away like that, so fast, no, that's impossible, there was knocking just now and I opened the door right after the last knock, and the person who was knocking can't have just disappeared, no, I don't believe it, that can't have happened, people don't do things like that, not people in Vaim anyway, and my goodness it's so dark out, even though it's so early in the day everything's almost totally dark, it's probably only around four o'clock in the afternoon and still it's so dark that you can't see anything, and well that's how it is at this time of year, just before Christmas, so if I don't see anyone I can always ask

  Is anybody there? I say

  and I don't hear anything, and I think that I should say it again

  Anybody there? I say

and it's not like I expect to get an answer, and I don't get any answer either, but where can the person who was knocking have disappeared to, he or she has to be somewhere, nothing else is possible, because thin air can't knock on a door, or can it, no, but the wind can shake and rattle a door or other things, that's true, but I heard so clearly that there was knocking, hard and for a long time, it was quiet and then there was another knock, but a careful one, no, I have to figure this out and I slip on my clogs and I go out the front door and I go over to the corner of the house, no, no one's there, could it maybe be someone playing a joke on me, but now who would do that, maybe some kids, but there aren't any kids living around here, there've been fewer and fewer children born in Vaim over the years, but now this is actually creepy, maybe it was a ghost, that's possible, yes, everything seems to point to it being a ghost that was knocking on the door, and I've never had any doubt that ghosts exist, even if I've never seen or heard one before today, but no, it can't have been a ghost, and so it must have been a person, because there's no animal that can knock like that on a door, no, and it can't have been the wind, because it's not windy now, there's no wind, so in that case – yes well what can it have been, it must have been a person, but I can't see anyone anywhere, and there's fresh snow too, so that means I can go look for footprints in the snow, I just need to go inside and get a torch and then walk around the house and see if I see footprints, and of course I need to check the road, or path I guess, that goes down to the main road, and then, yes I need to put on some warm clothes, because it's got cold outside, I think and I go inside and put on my big thick jacket and pull a cap down over my ears and then I take the torch that's hanging in its place in the hall and then I go right outside and I go around the house and I shine the light both ahead of me and to either side, but there aren't any footprints, not straight ahead of me and not to either side, and not on the road either, and it can't have snowed since the knocks, no of course not, and since there's no wind it can't be that snowdrifts have covered the footprints, no, I don't understand, whoever knocked on my door must have vanished into thin air as they say, it's strange, I can't understand it, I think, and it's cold outside so I guess I better go back in, this knocking is what it is, I think, most likely the knocking was just something I imagined, I think and I go to the front door and I stamp my feet to knock off the clumps of snow from my clogs, and then I realize that I need to turn off the torch, there's no reason to have it on in the light from the house, I think, I turn off the torch, knock the snow off my clogs, go into the hall, slip off my clogs, take off my jacket and cap, shut the front door, but this was really strange, I think, so I must just have heard wrong, heard something that wasn't there, just imagined that someone was knocking, yes maybe I felt so alone that I imagined someone knocking at my door, yes, that might be what happened, I can't think of any other reasonable explanation, but there, yes, there's a knock at the door again, and this, this isn't something I'm just imagining, that's a knock, and there's another knock, yes, not just knocking, yes, there's a real hammering on the door, yes, pounding, yes, it sounds almost like a thunderclap, no, not quite that bad, but almost, yes, almost like a thunderclap, but just almost, and there, there's another knock, but not quite as hard now, no, this, I think, no, I'm not imagining this, I'm really hearing it, there's no doubt about it, but now should I open the front door again even though I couldn't see anyone there the last time I opened the door, yes I probably should, I think and I go over to the door and now I hear something like a slow knocking and then, suddenly, I yank the door open and shout in an extremely irritated voice

Yes who is it?

and I almost leap right out the door I'm so surprised by my own voice and when I jump it feels like I'm breaking through some kind of gentle comfortable wall, or how can I put it, it's not warm or cold, and then I stood there outside the front door, all alone, and I looked all around, up, down, behind everything, but there was no one and nothing, no, this, I thought, no, I can't tell anybody this, not even Jatgeir, because they'll think I've gone crazy, because there's no way to believe that I've heard this, yes, it's probably like the people who heard voices and everyone thought they were crazy and sent them to The Madhouse in Bjørgvin, so I'm not going to say anything about this, not a word to anyone, I thought, but what could it have been, or who, that's a better way to put it, no, there was no way to understand it, it was inexplicable, as they say, it was actually spooky, yes, it was so frightening that I didn't really want to go back to my room, but I had to, I had to lie down for a bit on the bench and rest, I think and I go and lie down on the bench and spread the blanket over me and I think that it feels like I need someone to talk to, but I don't have too much contact with other people, well, yes, I had a little contact with my family, even that's tapered off too in recent years, after my parents died, those two sisters of mine never had all that much to do with me, to tell the truth, and then they got married and lived in other parts of the country, where the men they married came from, that's where they lived, each with her husband, and they'd had children too, one had two daughters, the other had a son, and then, the children, yes, I was these children's uncle but all of them were grown now, good and grown up, or almost grown up, and I wasn't in touch with my sisters much, so I hadn't had any contact at all with those two girls and that one boy I was uncle to, to tell the truth I wasn't even entirely sure of their names, yes well one was named Karen Elise, or maybe they wrote it Karen-Elise, if it wasn't Marte Elise actually, and then there was Gudrun Anna or Anna Gudrun, and there couldn't be a hyphen between Anna and Gudrun or Gudrun and Anna could there, no, I didn't think so, but I couldn't be sure of that either, and as for which of the two was named what I'd never managed to learn that, but the other sister had a son, and his name was Olaf, and that was easy to remember since he was named after my father, after my and my sisters' father, but his two sisters, my aunts, it was even worse with them, not that their names were so hard, they were Gudrun and Olaug, both fine names, and I knew that they were named after my father's parents, yes, my grandmother was named Olaug and my grandfather was named Gudmund, that's how it was, if I'm not remembering that all wrong, but even I couldn't be wrong about something like that, but I could never remember which one was Gudrun and which one was Olaug, no, but I usually managed to get through situations that could have been embarrassing by talking about both Olaug and Gudrun in general, but is that something I should be thinking about now, no, definitely not, certainly not after I heard a mysterious knocking at my door without there being anyone there knocking, no matter how long I tried to find them, and now I realize I'm feeling anxious, and I think I'll just go drop by Jatgeir's house, even if it's been a year and a day since the last time I did that, because to try to soothe this anxiety a little I'll just go and see him, this anxiety doesn't feel good at all, no, and to tell the truth it's been years now since I've visited Jatgeir and to tell the truth he's the only person in Vaim I ever visit, so if I'm going to do it again it might as well be now, to put it that way, but it kind of hasn't been the same since she, what was her name again, yes, Eline, right, since she came back with him on his boat after he'd taken his boat trip to Bjørgvin during the summer holiday like usual, the way he always used to do every summer, but many years back, yes, time goes by so fast that it's already many years ago now, he didn't come back home alone, no, that summer he brought a woman back with him, and not just any woman either, but someone who up until then, that's what people said anyway, was married and living on Sartor, but she'd grown up in Vaim and funnily enough the boat Jatgeir had had all those years was called the Eline, and maybe that was why the woman he brought back home was called Eline too, so now Jagteir was living with her, in sin, at least that's what some of the prayerhouse people said, and it was hard to believe Jatgeir would do something like that, come dragging some married woman back to Vaim who'd left Vaim a long time before, someone barely anyone in Vaim even remembered and wouldn't have remembered if it weren't for this going and kidnapping the bride, yes that's what they called it in the countryside, kidnapping the bride, people talked about how her husband might come to Vaim one day to get his wife back and he'd beat Jatgeir to death, or at least beat him up badly, because the man she was married to was surely a big strong man, and a fisherman on Sartor, or for all I knew he was just glad to get rid of his wife, that was another rumour going around, that that's how it was, it was probably one of the guys at The Quay below The Vaim General Store who'd said that maybe it was like that, and if only there was a meeting tonight in The Vaim Prayerhouse I could have some company there, but there wasn't, and I'd never gone to see anyone other than Jatgeir, for many years, earlier I used to go by and see him a lot, and Jatgeir would come see me at least as often, but ever since he's had a common-law partner, as they call it, yes, then it's like he wasn't the same anymore, so now it could go a year and a day between times that I saw him, not that she, yes, his partner, yes, Eline minded at all when I did stop by once, after such a long time, no, she retreated to the kitchen and then maybe poked her head out and asked if she could make us a cup of coffee or something and then Jatgeir said that might taste good and I said yes please, thanks, that'd be great, and then Jatgeir and I sat there and everything was like the old days, but only almost like it used to be, because everything was kind of completely different, it was like Jatgeir had become a different person somehow, even if he looked exactly like the same old Jatgeir, but something had changed, no question about it, he had become shy in a way he never used to be before, more withdrawn, like he had to be careful all the time and he couldn't just say whatever he wanted anymore, he had to think it over almost before he said anything, to make sure he didn't say anything that might be offensive, or whatever the term is, and the only thing I could think of that had changed was her, Eline, who had moved in with him, and even if she had come quietly and unnoticed her being there wouldn't have stayed unnoticed, if you can put it that way, because the living room was unrecognizable, the pile of old newspapers in the middle of the floor, old issues of *The Northern Herald*, the pile that had grown week after week, and would have filled up the whole room sooner or later, I'd thought, and driven Jatgeir out of his own living room, now the pile of newspapers was gone, and where multiple years' worth of newspapers had once stood there was now just a gaping void that you sort of couldn't help looking at the whole time, and then the curtains, they had been the same for all those years but now they'd been replaced by curtains with a pattern of large flowers in all kinds of colours, while the ones that had been there before had been brown, not even the sofa cushions were the same old cushions, and I just couldn't bring myself to ask where the old newspapers had gone, the old curtains, no, nothing was the way it was before and that meant I didn't really like going to visit him either, because he never came by to visit me anymore, but who else could I go see, probably no one, to tell the truth, so I'd probably better stay at home, I thought, and if I was going to go somewhere I'd have to wear good shoes and my nice warm coat, but it was probably best for me to just stay home, and not worry about whatever that knocking was, it was most likely just something I'd imagined, I thought and then I must have dozed off, because I woke up, and the first thing I thought about was that knocking there'd been on the door before I lay down, yes, I just couldn't understand it – but there was another knock, hard, yes, so hard it made me jump, I must have fallen asleep, I don't know for how long, and now a knocking suddenly woke me up, and I sat up on the bench, and now there was more knocking on the door, hard now too but not as hard as before, no, this, and I stand up and go out to the hall and there's another knock on the door, but now it's pretty soft, no, it was just something I was imagining, there's nothing else it could be, so now I won't open the door, if there'd been footprints in the snow I'd know for sure that there were just some kids playing a joke on me, that it was a prank, and now these kids had hidden somewhere or other and were laughing about how they'd tricked me, had even scared me, yes, but I guess that's fine, they could do that, there wasn't that much for kids in Vaim to do, probably the only fun they had was what they came up with themselves, but it's strange I hadn't thought of that before, that it was a kid, not a ghost, I must have turned into someone who's easily tricked and easily scared too, I'd started believing in all kinds of things, but there's another knock, and now as hard as can be, so I probably need to open the door again, and if there's no one there then at least I'll know that there are some rascals lurking in the dark somewhere giggling and snickering and having a good laugh about how they'd tricked me again, but this time they won't see me looking scared at least, they sure won't, not that, no, not this time, and there's another knock, a little harder than last time even, and now I'll open it right away, so, over to the door, yank it open – and look, but but can you believe it, if it's not Jatgeir himself standing there, no, who would believe it, I'm going around thinking that I should drop by Jatgeir's house and he must have been thinking the same thing, because if it isn't Jatgeir himself standing here in person

You must be surprised to see me, Jatgeir says

and I think that I probably can't say that I was just pacing around my living room thinking that I should go see him, and definitely not that there'd been a knocking and pounding and hammering on the door for a good long time and then when I went to open the door there was no one there, and that I'd got a bit anxious and scared and so I'd thought I'd go see my old friend

Come in, I say

I believe I will, he says

Come in old man, I say

and Jatgeir walks through the door and I say it's been a long time since we've seen each other, I honestly can't remember when the last time was, it's been so long, I say and Jatgeir says he'd almost say it must be several years and I say I can believe it and Jatgeir says no, he can't remember exactly when the last time was

No, our memory's not as good as it used to be, I say

True enough, he says

That's how things are with us, Elias, he says

Elias, Jatgeir says

Yes, I say

When I got here I saw someone standing outside your door, he says

Someone was standing outside my door, I say

Yes, yes, I saw someone there, I saw it when I came around the corner of the house, he says

and I don't say anything

And the strange thing was that he just suddenly disappeared, he says

It was a man, I say

No, I can't say for sure, but I'm sure that someone was standing there, he says

Really, I say

And it wasn't so strange that someone was there, the strange thing was that he suddenly disappeared, yes, vanished into thin air, he says

It was eerie, he says

Yes, I say

and I think about whether I should tell Jatgeir after all that there'd been the sound of knocking, yes, practically pounding on my door, and that it had scared me, but maybe the best thing would be to not tell anyone about that, probably, because then everything would just get even more frightening, I'd get even more anxious, or maybe not, because at least now I knew for certain that some kind of ghost had been at my door, there couldn't be any doubt about it now, or maybe there could, in some strange abstract way, abstract, yes, now that's a word to use in this situation, but a ghost probably is abstract if it exists at all, because you can't say it's concrete, can you, a spirit without a body in some way is probably what a ghost is, or however you'd say it, but it was weird that Jatgeir knocked on my door right afterwards, could it be that the knocking was a sign he was about to come, a warning, an omen, as they say, but can that really happen, for someone to, for example, knock before they actually come and knock, no, it can't be, things like that don't happen, but anyway Jatgeir's here now, but he needs to come in and not just stay standing in the doorway, I have to ask him again to come in and then I can offer him a cup of coffee

You'll take a cup of coffee, I say

and Jatgeir just looks at me

You're not scared of ghosts? he says

and I don't really know what to say, and Jatgeir sort of answers for me, no probably not really, he says and I can only nod in response

So that's how it is, Jatgeir says

and then it's quiet again, and suddenly, without warning, Jatgeir says that he has to go home

But you just got here, I say

Yes but there's something I forgot, he says

I just realized it, he says

So I'm going now, I have to hurry, he says

and I say that well anyone can forget something, but he should come by again soon, I say

But I actually just wanted to say a quick hello, he says

I need to hurry, he says

and I say I understand, yes, even though I don't understand anything he's saying, no

Talk to you soon, Jatgeir says

See you later, I say

and I see Jatgeir turn around and start to walk away

from the house, he's walking slowly, and then he sort of disappears around the corner of the house, and I stay where I am looking out the open door and for some reason I decide that I want to leave the door open, but I can't do that, it's cold outside and I can't leave the door open and let all the cold in, no, it'd be better if I took a walk, I'll just put on my warm coat and then my black sailor's cap, the one I always wear, and I don't exactly know why I've worn a black sailor's cap all these years, but there it is, so I'll put my things on and head out to The Vaim General Store, because it's probably open, but I can't think of anything I need to buy, still I can just take a walk over there, I think, since I don't know where else I could go, if there was a meeting at The Vaim Prayerhouse I'd have gone there, yes, I'd even go to Jatgeir's house, if he hadn't just been here, so if I want to see people I guess I'll just go to The Vaim General Store then, but on Sunday there's service at The Vaim Church, not that I'm a believer, but I go to the prayerhouse and the church anyway just to be with other people, and I'm kind of a believer too, in my way, and I look forward to going to church on Sundays, I think, so off I go to The Vaim General Store, because maybe I can talk a little with the guys who are usually there at The Quay, and then I'll probably remember some little thing I can buy, but I was just there to do my shopping a couple days ago so I can't think of anything I can buy today, but the guys at The Quay will definitely be there, at least some, today too, so I can probably talk to them for a bit, the way I sometimes do, not that often, I'm not one of the guys who hangs around there all the time, but I don't want to stay home anyway, I need to calm my nerves, as they say, so let's put on that sailor's cap and outer coat and these good solid shoes and then I'm off, yes, and I put them on and go out the door, and shut the front door behind me and then I walk down the side road to the country road and then I take a left and then go straight down to The Vaim General Store, no, I don't want to think about that knocking on the door, or that short visit from Jatgeir either, I think and without thinking about either thing I walk fast, because it's a cool night, and I try to think of something I can buy at The Vaim General Store, but I can't think of anything, so I don't even need to go into the store, I can just go down to The Quay and talk for a bit with the guys there, because over there, yes, there are some guys standing there the way there usually tend to be, and that's good, isn't it, because there isn't always someone there even if there usually is, but they don't look too talkative today, they're just standing there silently with their heads bent, not how they usually stand there, they usually stand there talking a little and usually laughing about this or that, so nothing's the way it usually is today, I think and then they hear me walking up and everyone looks up at me and then they look back down again and it doesn't look like any of them are going to say here comes our prayerhouse man today, or here comes our churchman, no, it doesn't look like any of them has anything at all to say today, but I'll probably still go over to them, there's nothing else I can really do since I'm already on my way towards the guys on The Quay, and I go down to them, I stop, don't say anything, and none of them looks at me, they just stand there looking down and now someone's got to say something

Not too chatty today are you, I say

and it takes a long time before one of them looks straight ahead instead of down

Yes, it's sad, he says

and I stand there and wonder what he means, what he's saying is sad

That he's gone, yes, he says

And you were such good friends, you and him, another one says

and again it's silent

What are you talking about, I say

and all the guys standing there, maybe four or five guys, look up and lean towards me

Yes, I say

That he's gone? I say

Yes, Jatgeir, he says

What do you mean? I say

Jatgeir died today, he says

and he looks at me not understanding

Jatgeir, I say

and no one says anything

You haven't heard? one of them says then

Heard what? I say

That Jatgeir died today, he says

and I shake my head

No, but, I say

He was found floating in the sea, dead, next to his boat, he says

I was just talking to him, yes, it can't have been more than half an hour ago, I say

and they look at me again, not understanding

But he was found several hours ago, drowned, one of them says

I just saw him, yes, I talked to him right before I came down here, and it's not that long a walk, I say

No, he was found a couple of hours ago, drowned, one of them says

She, yes, that common-law partner of his, right, she found him floating in the sea next to his motorboat, he says

And she couldn't manage to pull him back onto land, and then she found a rope and she tied him to the dock and then, he says

And then I came walking by, he says

And then she shouted I had to come help her, and when I went down there I saw Jatgeir lying there floating in the cold water with his nose pointing up in the air, he says

and again no one says anything and I think now that's too much for me, that's just too much, I don't understand anything in the world anymore, because I was just talking to Jatgeir, and he was as alive and well as ever, and didn't we talk about how I should visit him, no, we didn't talk about that, but still, I think

I was just talking to Jatgeir, I say

Yes, right before I came here, I say

Yes well then he rose up from the dead, one of them says

Yes like another Christ, he says

There's a lot you can accuse Jatgeir of, but he wasn't some other Christ, another one says

But you know more about that kind of thing than we do, a third one says

The doctor came and looked at him and declared him dead, there was nothing to do to try to save him, one says

and it's silent, totally silent, and my thoughts kind of go back and forth without them being thought, and I'm frozen in place, just standing there

Yes, the two of you were good friends, one says

Yes, I say

Yes, even if you were a prayerhouse person, Elias, and he sure wasn't, one says

and again it's silent, and I think that I probably can't just stay standing here, I have to keep going, whatever that means, I think

Yes, it's sad, one says

Very sad, another one says

And so unexpected, he says

Because he's spent his whole life on the water, another one says

I can't understand it, a third one says

No, I say

It's like there's nothing you can say about it, one says

and then what they're saying turns into a droning buzz of voices, and I can't tell the difference between what one of them is saying and what the others are saying, the words and the sentences blend into one another the same way my thoughts are blending into one another, and I was just talking to Jatgeir, but, no, I can't understand it, and then it probably was him who knocked on my door, yes, after he'd already drowned, yes, that's how it must have been, that's the only explanation, if I can call it an explanation, and it's spooky, I think, but why did he come by to talk to me after he was dead, yes, like back in the old days, as if nothing had changed, no, probably no one can understand things like that, I think, it was like he came to say goodbye, I think, and I guess I can't do anything but go back home now, because what else can I do then, I don't have anywhere else to go

Yes, okay, see you later, I say

and there's a sound like thanks you too or something like that from the guys there on The Quay and then I turn around and start to walk home

See you at the prayerhouse, one of them says behind me

Or in church, another one says

Yes and of course at Jatgeir's funeral, a third one says

and I think that it's unbelievable, but Jatgeir was a good person, and my only friend in Vaim, yes, probably the best friend I had in my whole adult life, and if he's gone now, yes, then he's gone, that's for certain, and as for what he believed or didn't believe, we never talked about that, and he probably never set foot in The Vaim Prayerhouse or The Vaim Church either, but what does that mean, no, I thought, and I thought that this drowning had something to do with Eline in a way, that he couldn't stand living with her anymore, that he got careless and fell into the sea because of that, either he was going to just check on his boat or he was going for a little ride, but if that was what happened then it should have really happened a long time ago because Eline had been living in his house for a year and a day, she just moved in, just did what she wanted, yes, that's really it, she got on board his boat some way or another, and Jatgeir couldn't get her off his boat, she was just there, on the boat and later in his house, and who knows, maybe it was because he'd named his boat Eline that she dared to do it, I didn't know, but why in the world had he named his boat Eline and then someone named Eline came on board and moved in with him, no, it was impossible to understand, I think, and I think that now I'll go straight home and then I'll pull myself together and pray for Jatgeir, I think, and I'll miss him, because if you could say I had any friend at all in Vaim it was Jatgeir, in all of Vaim his was the only house I've ever been in, and he was the only person who ever came through the door of my humble home, I never really got to know the people I met at The Vaim Prayerhouse and in The Vaim Church, and I probably won't ever get to know them either, but after this Eline moved in with Jatgeir, yes, it wasn't so nice to see him anymore, I kind of got the feeling that Eline didn't like me coming to visit, and she most likely didn't like Jatgeir coming to see me either and that's why he stopped coming over to my house, and I stopped going over to his house too, so it was not least because of that that it was such a surprise to see him standing outside my door today, and then this, yes, that he drowned today, and around the same time he was talking to me, no, it's unbelievable and you can't understand it either, but anyway he probably came over to say goodbye maybe, that's what must have happened, and now I have no one I can say I'm friends with in Vaim, there are just these prayerhouse people and church people left, but they don't really count since I've kind of never got to know them, we kind of just belonged to the same organizations and so now I'm even more alone than I've ever been before, and there, yes, there, I can feel that it's like Jatgeir's near me, but it's not that I can see him, and he seems happy and it's like he's waving goodbye and he says that it's good where he is now, and I feel like Jatgeir is looking down at me now from somewhere above me, but not that far above me, and I get the feeling that he now knows everything that's going to happen in the future, with me too, and he somehow takes it all in with a happy calm, and I could probably say in Christian words that he is in God's peace now and in the light of Christ's cross, but I feel like those are kind of just meaningless words and I raise my arm and I wave at him and it's like he raises his arm and waves at me and with a kind of joy he says it's good here, and I, walking up the road in Vaim, I raise my hand and wave at the sky, at where I feel like Jatgeir is, and everything feels right, but what would someone think if they saw me doing this, but after all there isn't anyone who can see me, yes, except for Jatgeir

Goodbye Jatgeir, I say

And thank you for our time together, I say

and I see Jatgeir, see his hand and arm, disappear into the dark sky

III

She called me Frank, from the first time we met she called me Frank – hi Frank, nice to see you, she said to me, or something like that, it was in Bjørgvin, it was at the restaurant called The Fowl where I'd gone with the two guys I fished with on the Elinor, the three of us did all kinds of fishing on that ship back then, and then it would sometimes happen that if we'd had a good catch and got a good price for the fish that we'd take a little trip to Bjørgvin, dock at one of the quays on The Wharf, spend a night there usually, getting in sometime in the afternoon and leaving at dawn or sometime the next morning, it depended how late a night we'd had, to tell the truth on how drunk we'd got, it was Eivind and Lars and me working on the ship then, an old ship that Eivind's father owned, but he'd been scared of the sea so he was rarely or never on board the Elinor, I didn't know why the ship had that name, Eivind had asked his father about it of course, but his father hadn't wanted to answer and refused to, a bit abruptly, one thing for sure anyway was that Eivind's mother, his father's wife, wasn't named Elinor, for whatever that's worth, but anyway Eivind's father got a full half share of what we made fishing since he owned the boat and the equipment, or maybe not quite half, we thought it was too much, more than was reasonable, so we usually rounded down a little, to put it that way, but anyway never mind that, when we'd had a good catch and had a lot of money to spend, yes, then we'd treat ourselves by paying a visit to a restaurant in Bjørgvin, and we always went to The Fowl, they had good country cooking there at a more reasonable price than the other places, the other places in Bjørgvin we knew of anyway, but to tell the truth there weren't that many, I probably hadn't, and probably haven't to this day, been to any other places in Bjørgvin besides The Fowl, and well I've been to The Bus Café and

The Coffeehouse, but those are probably the only places I've been, usually I always ended up at The Fowl, that's how it was with that, and that's what happened that day too, yes, the day I met Eline for the first time, and it happened quite simply like this, that Eline came over to the table where Eivind and Lars and I were sitting with our meatball dinners, she put both her hands on the edge of the table, looked straight at me, I don't remember exactly what she said to me, but she said Frank, hi Frank, nice to see you again, she said, it was something like that, so I guessed she must have made a mistake and thought I was someone else, or maybe she just said Frank because that's the name she came up with, I never dared to ask her about it even though she kept calling me Frank for the rest of her life, but still I looked up at her, I must have, but I don't remember what I said, maybe I didn't say anything, but I remember that either Eivind or Lars said that actually my name wasn't Frank, my name was something totally different, my name was Olaf, nothing else, just Olaf pure and simple, but this woman who'd come over to our table, and who was now standing there clutching the edge of the table, maybe because she'd had a bit too much to drink and so had to hold herself up, she didn't listen, she looked me straight in the eye and said something that implied that she knew me, yes, that we knew each other well, we were old friends, or long-time acquaintances anyway, but I couldn't remember having ever seen her before, of course it was possible that I'd drunk so much the time we met that I couldn't remember meeting her, but that wasn't really very likely, it was true enough that I did have a bit to drink sometimes, quite a lot sometimes, yes, but I was rarely or never as drunk as all that, no, and there she stood looking at me, yes, and I was seeing her for the first time, that I could remember at least, yes, it was a long time since I'd drunk enough to not remember what happened, things like that happened only when I was really young, and only a couple of times then, before I learned to eat enough and not overdo the drinking, but on that day, at The Fowl, the day Eline stood there at our table, pretty drunk even though it was a weekday, and called me Frank, and wouldn't stop, she had decided my name was Frank and so that was my name, nothing to discuss, I was Frank, and in all the years we eventually lived together she never once called me Olaf, only Frank, and I have to admit that it took me a long time to get used to also being called Frank, as well as Olaf, to tell the truth I never really got used to it, and that wasn't so strange since she was the only person who called me Frank, everyone else used my real name, Olaf, no more, no less, Olaf pure and simple, but actually it was fine to be called Frank too, I got used to it, so it was no wonder that people in Sund started calling me Frank-Olaf, or Olaf-Frank, and calling her, Eline, Franka, or sometimes Frenka, or Frenke-Franka or Franke-Frenke, almost no one ever used her actual name, Eline, neither in Sund nor in Vaim, she mostly went by Frenka, or Franke-Frenka, probably no one, yes, except me, ever called her Eline, and actually it was pretty rude that they never called her Eline, her real name, although actually her birth name was Josephine, she told me that once, privately, and that's the name on her tombstone, so there aren't many people, aside from the few so to speak initiates, yes, actually maybe just the few people who came to her funeral, where the pastor used her real name, Josephine, who know what Eline's, or Frenka's, or Franke-Frenka's real name was, and even in Vaim they completely stopped calling her Eline, same as in Sund, or they called her Eline as long as she lived with Jatgeir, or the man called that, even though his real name was Geir, pure and simple, and they faithfully called her Eline too for the first couple of years after he passed away, but ever since the two of us were living together, and after they found out in Vaim that my birth name was Olaf but that everyone in Sund called me Frank, yes, then everyone called me that in Vaim too, but it was back at The Fowl, on that day many many years ago, that I was so to speak rebaptized Frank, and with Eivind and Lars as witnesses, or godfathers, I could probably say – Frank, so I'm Frank now, might as well get used to it, even if I don't recognize myself in that name, the way I did in the name Olaf, when I went by Olaf, the name my parents gave me, but now Eline, still standing there, has asked me if I want to dance

Would you care to dance, Frank, she said

and even though I was sitting there with a plate of meatballs I hadn't finished I couldn't very well say anything other than yes, because the band, it must have been Hungarian or something like that, was playing their music and it was a waltz too, and if I was going to try to dance anything it would have to be a waltz, not that I could waltz, but I certainly couldn't do any other dance, so if I was ever going to dance it was going to be now, even though that wasn't really the way it was supposed to be, the woman asking the man to dance, it was supposed to be the man who asked, that was a long-standing rule, but to tell the truth I had never once done that, asked someone to dance, yes, or actually I did once, but I probably lost the will to try again when the woman I asked got an angry look on her face and said no as loud as she could so that as many people as possible could hear it, she said no, and I can still see her face before my eyes today, how she looked up, leaned back a little, looked right at me and then said no and that no didn't come from someone who was asked to dance all that often, it came from someone who most likely was going to be left there forgotten, and maybe that was exactly why she rejected me so loudly and harshly, so that no one would think she was sitting alone because she didn't have any suitors, but it sure threw cold water on things and so there weren't too many times I'd been on the dance floor, probably the first time was a school dance where a teacher tried to teach us all to waltz at least, yes, that's how it was, I remember now, that's how I learned a few waltz steps, and then and there, that time I was sitting and eating meatballs with Eivind and Lars at The Fowl it came in handy, because the band was playing its best, and this woman standing there holding the edge of the table and asking me to dance and who clearly thought I was someone else, someone she knew, yes, she clearly wasn't going to take no for an answer, so there was really only one thing to do, leave my meatballs sitting there and get onto my feet and dance a waltz as best I could, and I stood up and then she pulled me by my shirt sleeve, I had taken off my jacket and hung it on the back of the chair, she pulled me onto the dance floor, where no one else was dancing, there was just the band playing its best, kind of like they were half asleep, but now they sort of woke up, the drummer hit his drums harder, the bassist thumped his strings more clearly and The Blue Danube Waltz filled the whole dance floor, even if no dancers did, and she said to me now just dance as well as you can, Frank, and then she took my right hand and pulled it, and she put her arm around my waist, and I put my left arm around her waist, and it was slim, and soft, and it sure felt good to have my hand there, and then she pulled me into the dance, it was she who led, and I followed as well as I could, and I thought it was going pretty well, but then she put her mouth up to my ear and said, kind of loud

    You dance like an ox, she said

and I didn't know what I could say to that
But you're a good-looking guy, she said
Maybe you and me can be a couple, she said

and then we kept dancing, and I, who hadn't thought I was dancing that badly, I look over at the table where Eivind and Lars are sitting and they're laughing and clapping and no, no, this isn't going well at all, I think, I'm just being laughed at, but luckily there aren't many people in The Fowl now, it's the middle of the week, and early, and that's good, and I look at the band and no, that's not a little laugh I see behind those faces not looking at anything, is it, yes, it is, they're just pretending like they don't see me, but every last one of them is looking right at me and thinking whatever they're thinking, and at the same time they must be happy that someone's dancing, because it can't be much fun to play dance music when no one's dancing, not for long anyway, and then The Blue Danube ends and I take my hand off her waist, but she keeps her hand on my waist and doesn't let go of my right hand

Thanks for the dance, I say

and she doesn't say anything to that, and I'd thought I should say that, say thanks for the dance, but maybe that wasn't the right thing to say

Frank, Frank, she says

and I don't really know what I can say to that, there's no point in saying my name isn't Frank, that would probably just start some kind of argument, but maybe I can ask her what her name is

My name's Eline, she says
and I think she must be able to read minds too
And maybe you and me can be a couple, she says
and I can't believe what I'm hearing
Yes, let's sit down and talk a little, she says
My table's over there, she says

and she points and I see a round table with a pint glass on it and a suitcase on the floor next to the table, and she pulls me over to the table and she points at one chair and says I should sit there and she'll go get my pint, and as soon as she's said that I see her dash over, and she's quick, to the table where Eivind and Lars are sitting and she takes my pint and is already heading back to me and the band has started playing another waltz, they must have felt that a waltz was the thing after their success with The Blue Danube and she comes hurrying over to me in a waltz rhythm and then she's standing right in front of me holding my pint

Have a seat, she says

Okay, I say

and I sit down in the chair she'd pointed out for me and she puts my pint down in front of me, opposite hers, and then she trots over and gets my jacket and hangs it on the back of my chair, and she sits down where her pint is and takes a sip and I think what in the world am I doing and getting myself into

Frank, Frank, she says

It's so nice to see you, yes, she says

and I don't know what to say, but one thing's for sure and certain, she thinks we've met before

But have we met before, I say

Well, no, she says

But we can always get to know each other, she says

Okay, I say

Yes definitely, she says

But skoal, she says

and she lifts her pint and I lift mine and the glasses clink together

To good health, and happiness, she says

And to a long life, she says

    To a long life together, she says
    and I think what in the world can she mean by saying that
    Prosperous and happy, she says
    Yes, Eline and Frank, she says
    and I think that there's no real point in saying that my name is Olaf, she'll just keep calling me Frank anyway
    You and me, Frank, she says
    and then she asks where I live and why I'm in Bjørgvin and I say that I'm a fisherman from Sund on Sartor and we'd had a good catch and had money in our pockets and that's why we took a little trip to Bjørgvin, the ship was moored at The Wharf, and she asked why I was at The Fowl in particular and before I could answer she asked if there was a lot of room in the house where I lived and for some reason or another I say that I inherited it from my parents and she says that that's sad, that my parents have passed away, that I'd been orphaned at such a young age and I go on to say that I don't have any brothers or sisters and she says it must be very lonely living alone like that in my childhood home after my parents have died, but now that I've met her I won't be lonely anymore, and she'd guess that my house isn't in good shape, how long has it been since I'd cleaned it, the floor, the stairs, never mind the walls, or the roof, and my diet couldn't be much to brag about if you looked at how skinny I was, so tall and skinny and practically lanky, but now, yes, now it'd be taken care of, yes, she'd look after all that, starting tomorrow, she said and I see Eivind come walking over to the table where we're sitting and that's good, I can stop sitting here alone talking to this Eline woman and Eivind is over by the table and he asks wouldn't I, wouldn't we, like to come back to the table where he and Lars are sitting and the woman Eline says no, we'll stay at this table, she and

I will, and Eivind says all right then yes okay, he didn't mean anything bad by it, he says and he turns around and is about to go back to the table where Lars is sitting by himself now and then she, Eline, says he should wait, she has something she wants to talk to him about and Eivind stops and looks at Eline

Yes, he says

Yes, go ahead, he says

Okay, Eline says

You, she says

Yes, he says

You'd better be heading back to Sartor tonight, to Sund, yes, once we're done drinking we'll go back to your ship, what's it called?

Elinor, Eivind says

That's a good name, it's like Eline, she says

Yes, that's my name, she says

Eline, yes, she says

So that's what you have in mind, Eivind says

And you have something else in mind, Eline says

We were planning to celebrate, Eivind says

Because we've had a good catch and have lots of money on us, he says

And now you want to drink it all up or something, she says

We made more than we could drink up, he says

and she points at the table where Lars is now sitting by himself

Now you go back to the table over there and finish your drink, and your friend can do the same, the one sitting there all by his lonesome, she says

and she asks if he too, yes, the one sitting by himself there, if he's a fisherman too, on the Elinor, yes, and Eivind says yes, that he himself is and that Lars, the one sitting by himself at the table, that's his name, is too, and then him, Olaf, that's the crew, he says

    You mean Frank, she says

    and Eivind looks at me and he looks resigned

    Yes okay, he says

    Okay now do what I said, she says

    Finish your drink, she says

    Finish your drink and then we'll go on board and then leave for Sartor right away, it's not far, she says

    But, Eivind says

    No buts, she says

    and Eivind looks at me and shakes his head

    Now do what I say, she says

    and I see Eivind go over to the table where Lars is sitting and she says now we need to drink up, and she empties her pint glass in one long sip

    Now you need to finish your drink too, she says

    and I raise my pint to my mouth and finish it in one sip and I see that she, Eline, has already stood up and picked up her suitcase and she says that actually she's from Vaim, but she was dumb and she moved, or she should probably say took a trip, to Bjørgvin, and she should never have done that, because Bjørgvin is no place to live, no place for normal people to live, just for swindlers, all the wealth in Bjørgvin is just what they've stolen from Strileland, she says, and that's exactly why all the Bjørgvin people look down on the Strilelanders, to the Bjørgvin people the Strilelanders aren't people at all, they're not human beings, just servants, workers, people who do things that the Bjørgvin people have to pay them some pathetic wage for and then they get it right back by what they make them pay for something little, yes, like a pint of beer at The Fowl, it costs her almost a half day's wages to get one pint at The Fowl, so that's enough beer drinking for now, she herself shouldn't have any more either, she says and she takes my upper arm and gently pulls me up from the chair and she says I need to take my jacket, and I do that, and she takes me under the arm and with me in one hand and the suitcase in the other hand she walks, or rather we walk, over to the table where Eivind and Lars are sitting and they're looking at us surprised, and once we're at the table she, Eline, says that we, yes, she says we, have decided that she'll come along on the ship back to Sartor, to Sund, and that they should finish their drinks now and that we'd all go back to the ship, yes, Elinor was its name right, yes, she hadn't introduced herself properly but her name was Eline, so the ship was practically named after her, yes, it sounded almost the same, she said and then she let go of my arm and held out her hand to Eivind and he stood up, shook her hand, said his name, and she held out her hand to Lars, and he stood up, said his name and when he started to sit back down Eline said that we, she really said we, yes, we had decided that the best thing to do would be to go to the ship now and without delay, that's exactly what she said, now and without delay, and Lars looked at Eivind who had already stood up and who now picked up his pint and drank it up and Lars picked up his and emptied it, and then they took their jackets, they were suit jackets, because we'd dressed up nice to go to The Fowl, each in a suit, with a white shirt and tie, and then Eline took me under the arm and we left The Fowl and Eivind and Lars were right behind us and I kind of felt the eyes of the band members on my back, and then, right then, they switched tunes and started playing something that you'd have to call a bridal march, no, this was too embarrassing, now we had to get out of there, quicker than quick, I thought, and we left, and then we were standing there on the pavement and I saw Eivind and

Lars start to walk down the pavement in the direction of
The Wharf and we, Eline and I, followed them

No, just think, we're a couple now, Eline said

I can't believe it, she said

You and me, Frank and me, she said

Frank and Eline, she said

and I didn't say anything, of course

You're not saying anything, Eline said

Tell me a story, she said

About what, I said

Yes, about our future, for example, she said

and I didn't say anything

Or maybe you can ask me something, about where I'm from, for example, but I guess I've told you that, Eline said

Where are you from, I said

I'm from Vaim, she said

But I already told you that, she said

So, you're from Vaim, I said

Is there anything wrong with that, she said

and we walked behind Eivind and Lars and I thought that this, no, I didn't understand a thing about what was happening, not one thing in the world

Have you ever been to Vaim, she said

Yes, barely, I said

What does that mean, she said

Yes just to The Vaim General Store once, I said

You were fishing near there, she said

Yes, I said

and I had no idea at the time, walking there, that I would end up living in Vaim, the way I eventually did, and going to The Vaim General Store at least once a week if not more, and maybe it was just as well that I didn't know what would happen, yes, all of it, good and bad, I think, yes, for sure and certain, it was probably for the best that I didn't know what awaited me, strange as it was, yes, all was strange, I've thought that so many times, all was strange, yes, that's what I hope they put on my tombstone, that's how my life should be summed up, as they say, let it be with the words All was strange, but Eline didn't want anything written on her tombstone, just the year she was born and the year she died, and then her name, but she did want, and she told me so a long time before she died, to be buried as close to Jatgeir as possible, so there couldn't have been any bad blood between them anyway, and I arranged it so that Eline could rest in peace as close to Jatgeir as possible, but she couldn't be right next to him, because that's where Elias had found his last resting place, he must have been the only person in Vaim that Jatgeir had been friends with, and the two of them must have seen each other a lot, visited each other, or sometimes anyway, that's what people said anyway, yes, it was Eline who told me that, and she didn't much like that Elias had been buried right next to Jatgeir, she had never really understood him, that Elias, he was a prayerhouse person, she'd said, and he went to church every time there was any service at The Vaim Church, so she'd never really understood how he and Jatgeir could get along so well, yes, and every time Elias dropped by, which was not actually that many times, maybe just a couple, yes, after she moved in with Jatgeir, yes, it seemed like he didn't like her, yes, basically like he was judging her, yes, condemning her for living in sin with Jatgeir, yes, that's the kind of thing they still said, or thought anyway, those prayerhouse people, yes, but, yes, he came over only a couple of times, and that was when she'd just recently moved there, and then he totally stopped coming over, and since she also didn't like it when Jatgeir went to see Elias, yes, they'd had little or nothing to do with each other since then, and for him, Elias, to dislike her, yes, judge her, he of all people, he who lived in a ramshackle little house and who'd probably never done a good day's work in his whole life, the government still paid him something every month for some unknown reason, and then for him to judge her and think she was living in sin, no, that was too much, but then he died not long after Jatgeir, so it was Elias, not her, who was buried next to Jatgeir, and that was a terrible torment to her, because then she couldn't rest there, she'd said, then her grave couldn't be next to Jatgeir's, but she still wanted to lie as close to Jatgeir as possible, even if Elias was going to lie between her and Jatgeir anyway, and that's how it was, she got a grave next to Elias and on his other side lay Jatgeir, and then she said that no matter where she was laid to rest, that's what she said, her real name Josephine should be on the tombstone, because no one knew that name and so no one would know that she was the one lying there since no one had used her birth name so it was really probably only me, most likely, who knew who was resting under that stone – and so I was left alone and I would go on one trip a week, either in the motorboat Eline, yes, I didn't just take over Jatgeir's house, yes, his childhood home, but also his motorboat, and everything else he owned, because Eline had arranged it so that she would inherit everything from Jatgeir, he didn't have any children after all, and only distant relatives, maybe they should have got something, I don't know, but in any case Eline ended up getting it all, and as far as I knew no one ever asked about getting any inheritance, and if I know Eline they wouldn't have got it either even if they had asked, yes, the bailiff would have had to come take it, but anyway everything stayed where it was, the motorboat Eline too, so for several years there were two boats called Eline docked at the quay, Jatgeir's motorboat and my sjark, yes, that's how it was until I sold the motorboat cheap to someone who just called himself The Sailor, who lived on a little island, he said he'd been looking at that motorboat for a long time and thought it was a very fine boat, so if I wanted to sell it he would be happy to buy it and what was I going to do with two boats anyway, to tell the truth it had been more of an obligation to take care of the motorboat, so I accepted his offer and it was a great day when I got rid of that motorboat, yes, the same way it had been a great day when I got the sjark, or at least it should have been a great day, I'd been fishing with Eivind and Lars on the Elinor for several years, but I thought that as soon as I'd saved up enough money to afford it I would buy myself a boat of my own, a sjark, yes, so that's what I did, no sooner said than done, and the guy who sold me the boat came with it himself, it was the day after Eline had decided that she couldn't stand me anymore and disappeared and left behind only a short letter, yes, the seller came with the sjark the day after Eline left, it was a guy from up in the Hardanger Fjord who sold me the boat, he came in the boat I'd bought and a friend came too, in another boat, and after I got the first boat the two of them went in the second boat back where they'd come from up in Hardanger Fjord, there wasn't enough of a profit if they each operated their own sjark, the guy who'd sold me the boat said, but if they shared one boat they could maybe make a living, the profit would have to be better than if they were paying the expenses on two boats anyway, so now the guy who'd sold me the boat was going to buy into the other boat, buy a share, and that would let them pay off the loan on it, and that by itself would make it much easier to get by, because this fjord fishing really didn't bring in much money, the guy who'd sold me the sjark said and he was clearly very happy that he'd sold the boat and I was no less happy that I'd bought the boat, but that was that, and it wasn't only just that, that's for sure, because when I'd got home from the sea the night before I got the sjark, that I'd decided to call Eline, and I'd already got a nameplate for it, it would be on the front of the wheelhouse in the middle in big black letters on brown enamel, Elinc, there was that letter from Eline sitting on the kitchen table, she'd written that she couldn't stand this life anymore and she'd gone away, she'd just taken her suitcase with the most necessary things she owned, so I didn't need to worry that anything important to me was gone, and since I clearly cared so little about her, yes, she didn't see any reason to say where she was going, I could probably guess, she wrote and I thought that she had come into my life in an unusual way and had left my life in an unusual way too, that's how it was now, but I missed her, a lot, but getting the boat I'd been so happy to get, yes, that probably made the separation easier, or at least made me not think about Eline as much as I would have if I hadn't got the sjark Eline, yes, there's no doubt I probably thought more about the sjark Eline than about Eline, and the very next day I mounted the letters of the name Eline on the front of the wheelhouse, yes, I probably have to admit that it felt a bit odd to do that, to mount the name Eline on my new boat the day after the real Eline had so suddenly and unexpectedly left me, but that's how it was, now Eline had gone her way, but at least I still had the sjark Eline and, if I thought about it, I wasn't entirely sure which of the two I would choose if I'd had the choice, or actually I was sure, I would've chosen the boat, and if that's how it was then it probably made sense that Eline would go on her way, but how had she left, and where, yes, I thought that over a lot, but when we were coming into shore on the Elinor the night she left I remembered that we'd seen a motorboat, yes, just before we got to shore, I was standing on the bridge and I saw that it said Eline on the side of the wheelhouse of the motorboat, and now that's strange I thought as soon as I saw that, yes, that the motorboat should have the same name as the woman I lived with and the same name that I had decided to name my sjark the next day too, but I didn't think that much about it and eventually I started wondering if I'd really seen the name Eline there on the side of the motorboat's wheelhouse, or if it was just something I'd imagined, but sure enough, I definitely thought a lot about Eline, and about where she'd gone, and about how she'd got there, but anyway I heard that a guy had moored his motorboat to the quay the day Eline left, and the boat was called Eline, it was The Shopkeeper at The Grocery Store who told me that, who'd worked there for many years, and who lived in a little apartment above the store, and she'd cheated him badly that day, because he'd asked for a needle and a spool of black thread to sew a loose button back on and she'd asked a price beyond all reason for the needle and thread, pretending like it was nothing, yes, like that was just the price, and would you believe it, she laughed and shrieked when she told me, and she told me again and again, that he'd bought the needle and thread, she had never made such a good sale in her life, not before and not since, she'd got two hundred and fifty kroner for it and one day she told me that she'd seen Eline go down to the quay that same night and she'd seen her go on board the motorboat docked there, it was still the day before I got the sjark and when she'd locked up The Grocery Store and taken a walk down to the quay she couldn't help but see that the nameplate on the side of the wheelhouse there said Eline, she said, so Eline had probably skipped out in the motorboat Eline, and most likely with the man who owned the motorboat and he was a good-looking middle-aged man, he must have been from somewhere in Sygne County judging from his accent, cleverly done wasn't it, but hardly a crime, hardly something a person would try to interfere with, she'd said and since I had seen that motorboat myself when we came into The Bay on the Elinor the night Eline left, and then passed a motorboat that was called Eline, yes, I felt sure I knew how she had left, but that it all would end with me eventually moving away from my childhood home, away from Sund, off Sartor, to live with Eline in Vaim, no, I never would have believed that, that I would move in with the woman who'd left me and live with her in Vaim, and in Jatgeir's house, the house of the man she'd gone with when she left me, no, you almost wouldn't think it was possible, that I'd gone along with that, that I'd accepted that, but once Eline decided something that was how it was going to be, yes, because one night when I was sitting in the good chair in my living room, after a long day on the water and so tired that I was about to fall asleep and thought I needed to go lie down, yes, there was a knock at the door, yes, a knock, and it had been a year and a day since the last time anyone had knocked on the door to my house, so who could it be? and should I open the door, I probably had to, because that was the custom in the countryside, to open the door when someone knocks, so I probably had to even though I was so tired, and really it was probably just some kid selling raffle tickets for some Christian cause or another who was knocking, one thing for sure was that no one else ever knocked, it never happened, no, I thought and I opened the door – and no, no, I couldn't believe my eyes, because there, in a coat, carrying a handbag, there stood Eline herself, how many years had it been since the last time I'd seen her, I couldn't remember just then but it was a long time, many years

   So can I come in, Eline said

   Yes, yes, I said

   But you didn't invite me in right away, she says

   Yes well, I say

   Thanks very much, Eline says

and she steps inside and she turns around and locks the door as if the last time she'd done it was just yesterday, and she walks into the hall and she hangs her coat up as if as if she'd done it just yesterday, and she goes into the living room

   Yes, everything here is just like it was, she says

   You haven't changed a thing as far as I can tell, she says

   After all these years, she says

and then I see her go into the kitchen and of course she moans and groans and says what a messy filthy kitchen, no, it's just out and out unbelievable, if she's going to say what she thinks it doesn't look like anything here has been cleaned and tidied up since the last time she did it, she says and she says this is no way to live

   Even if you are a fisherman you still need to live like a human being, Frank, she says

   and there it was again, that name, Frank, I hadn't heard that name since Eline just up and disappeared, or almost since then, but here it was so loud and clear that it resounded both in the living room and in my head

   Frank, Frank, she says

and I want to say that my name's not Frank, but there's no point

   I should have cleaned the place and tidied up but we need to go now, Eline says

   Go? I say

   Yes, she says

   Yes, now and without delay, she says

But, I say

No buts, she says

But where are we going? I say

You just take what you need and we'll go down to your boat, she says

To my boat? I say

You must still have the boat, yes, that sjark you bought? she says

Yes, the boat that was going to be named Eline, she says

Yes, but, I say

Take only what you need, lock up here, and we'll go down to the boat, she says

Yes, the boat, your sjark, must be called Eline for a reason, she says

and I don't answer and I understand little or nothing about what's happening but even so I understand that there's no arguing with Eline, life has taught me that much at least, but this, yes, this, no, I don't know what to say, I don't know what to think, and I don't understand what Eline has in mind, but I guess I just need to do what she says, it's probably not open to discussion, I think and I probably don't need to take all that much with me, I'm used to spending the night on the boat so I already have everything I need there, all the necessities, so really it's probably just my wallet and then the bankbook that I need to take, I think and I go to put on my coat and my wallet is in an inside pocket of the coat, and I have my bankbook in a drawer of my nightstand and I go upstairs and get it and I go back into the living room and then I see Eline standing there taking down the painting above the sofa and she says that the whole time she lived here she loved that painting so much, and to tell the truth, and she sure could do that, this painting was the only thing she missed after she'd left here, and now that didn't totally make sense, because the painting wasn't anything so special, it was just a picture of a sailboat at full sail, a jakt, but she'd never thought it was that pretty, and it was hanging there above the sofa for as long as I can remember, it was a picture of my great-grandfather's jakt, a proud vessel, with sails on both masts, and with the name Matilde painted on both sides of the hull at the bow and on the front of the wheelhouse, the wheelhouse was aft the way they usually were on boats like that, it was a handsome boat, it had made the trip up to Nordland and carried dried cod from Lofoten down to Bjørgvin, and my great-grandfather had made good money doing that, and with some of the money he had built a house I lived in while I was doing my military service, and my parents and grandparents had lived there too, and my great-grandfather's name was Olaf, the same as my father, and my grandfather, and that was my name too, so as long as my father was alive my mother called me Olaf-Olaf and called my father just Olaf, that's how it was and Eline asks what I'm standing there thinking about and I say that I wasn't thinking about anything in particular and Eline says that she knows me so well that she can see what I'm thinking about just by looking at me and I think that I won't ask her what she thinks I was thinking and she says that she knows I'm thinking about the jakt my great-grandfather owned in the painting and then I thought that that painting had hung there all these years and that it was almost a shame to take it down from the wall since it must have been hanging there ever since my great-grandfather had hung it there once a long time ago and I say well I was thinking something like that and Eline says that she can't count how many times I've told her about that painting, about how it's my great-grandfather's jakt portrayed in the picture and no, she doesn't want to hear me tell her about it over and over again, but it is a beautiful painting, so we need to bring it with us to Vaim now that we're going to live there, she says, and I stand there in shock, I'm supposed to live in Vaim now, what kind of an idea is that

Now we'll go down to your boat and then we'll head to Vaim, she says

To Vaim, on the boat? I say

Yes, right away, she says

But, I say

No buts, she says

and she's already on her way to the hall door

I'll go outside and wait and you come once you've turned off the heaters and the lights, and yes, yes, got what you most need to take, yes, yes, like I said, she says

and I say I'll do that and I think that this is totally incomprehensible, but it's like I have no choice, no will of my own, because once Eline has decided something, yes, then it's just going to happen like she says, yes, just like that day back at The Fowl, yes, she was sitting there with a suitcase and in it was everything she owned and I saw her standing there at The Wharf and I stood there on the deck of the Elinor with my arm reaching out to take her suitcase but she didn't hand it to me

I can manage the suitcase myself, she said

and I mumbled something like how I never thought she couldn't, and Eline climbed up over the railing and then she was standing there on deck and I understood little or nothing of what had happened, just as little as I understood now

Now go and get your suitcase and pack your things, what you need, she says

and I hurried upstairs and my good old suitcase was standing in the wardrobe and I took it out and I didn't really know what I should pack and take with me, it wasn't clear how long I'd be away, but I could probably take my suit and tie and nice shirt, so I put those in the suitcase, and if I was bringing nice clothes then my best shoes could probably come with, yes, so I put them in the suitcase too, and then a few pairs of wool socks, and then the good warm Icelandic jumper that was in there, and I probably didn't need to bring any more than that, it was probably just for appearance's sake and because Eline had asked me to get my suitcase that I was bringing it at all, because no I didn't know what I was actually doing now, and so I didn't know what I should bring with me either, and then I hear Eline calling that I should come, it shouldn't take all the time in the world just to pack a suitcase, she says and I say I'm coming

Can't you hurry it up a little, Eline says

I'm doing it as fast as I can, I say

Yes yes, Eline says

and I go downstairs and I see Eline standing in the hall like she's ready to leave

You're already ready to leave, I say

Yes, well, Eline says

But first you need to turn off the lights and the heaters and make sure all the doors are locked, she says

and I go down into the hall and put my suitcase down and then I open the door to the basement stairs, turn on the light and go down into the basement, turn on the light there and walk around the basement, and everything there is like it always is, and I check the basement door and it too is locked like it always is, and I turn off the light in the basement, go up the stairs, open the door to the hall, turn off the basement stairs light and go into the hall

Everything was fine and the door was locked, Eline says

Yes, yes, I say

And you've turned off all the lights and heaters upstairs too, she says

I think so, I say

It's not enough to just think so, Eline says

and I go upstairs again, and the lights in all the rooms are turned off and all the heaters are turned off, but really I knew that everything would be like that, so why in the world did I go upstairs to check, yes well it was purely and simply because Eline told me to, I think and then I'm back downstairs in the hall next to my packed suitcase

And so now we'll go, Eline says

I checked all the heaters down here and turned off all the lights, she says

and Eline has already opened the front door and is standing there in the entryway with two shopping bags in one hand and a handbag in the other

Come on now, she says

And bring the painting, she says

and she points to one of the walls in the entryway and I put on my good outer coat and pick up the suitcase, take the painting and put it under the arm I'm holding the suitcase with

And you had some food, not much, that I'll bring with, Eline says

and she lifts the shopping bags a little higher for a second

Just two bags, she says

and I turn off the light in the hall and go out into the entryway, take the keys out of my pocket and lock the front door and then Eline says I need to turn off the outside light and I unlock the door again, open the door, turn off the outside light and shut the door and lock it again and I see Eline start walking down the road, with shopping bags in one hand and a handbag in the other, and then I start walking after her, hauling the suitcase and the painting of my great-grandfather's ship, the jakt Matilde, and I walk the same speed as Eline, ten or twenty feet behind her, and I don't want to go faster, I don't want to get closer to her, it's better to keep a little distance, maybe then I can get clearer in my thoughts, because what is actually happening now, I'm walking here, with my suitcase, ten or twenty feet behind Eline, and we're obviously going down to my boat, the boat that by mistake, let's say, I named Eline and weirdly it was delivered the day after Eline had decided to go on her way the night before, leaving me nothing but a note that was hard to understand, she left as suddenly as she'd come, and now she'd just as suddenly come back again, I think, and I see Eline get on board the sjark with those two shopping bags and her handbag, and I get on board after her with my suitcase, and the painting, I put them down on the deck, the painting leaning against the suitcase, and now it's time to ask Eline what all this is supposed to mean, I think

So now what, I say

Well isn't that rude, Eline says

I didn't mean it in a rude way, I say

So now you'll start the boat and I'll untie the lines and then we'll go to Vaim, Eline says

To Vaim, I say

Yes I already said all that, Eline says

Why in the world am I going to Vaim, I say

You're going to live there, Eline says

Live there? I say

Yes, she says

But what'll I do there, I say

You'll fish, you'll be a fisherman just like before, she says

and she says that the Vaim Fjord is full of fish, not to

mention out in the ocean, she says, if I want to venture out into the open sea

But my fishing equipment, I say

There's more than enough equipment that Jatgeir left, in his boathouse, Eline says

Jatgeir, I say

Yes, the man I lived with, she says

and it's like everything becomes clear to me all at once, she left me with Jatgeir, in his motorboat, that night lord knows how many years ago, and now he was dead and now I was supposed to be her husband again in a way, and not least importantly be her breadwinner, the way it used to be all those years ago

So Jatgeir's dead, I say

He died a while ago, she says

And now I live alone in the house, she says

You need to start the engine, she says

and I go into the wheelhouse, take the key out of my pocket, put it in the starter, I start the engine and it starts first try like always and I see that Eline has unmoored both lines and now she's bringing the fenders on board, yes, I guess I'll just set my course north, I think and the sjark Eline glides away from the shore in the calm water, and it's like a kind of peace comes over everything, I think and without saying much we head north at a steady cruising speed, we're both quiet, to tell the truth it's like a solemn occasion all of a sudden, I think, and I sit and think about why Eline went away so suddenly, and left me just a short brusque letter on the kitchen table, she kind of just threw it down there, and she left the front door unlocked behind her, she'd probably been in too much of a hurry to lock the door, so it was quite the departure, I think and the sjark Eline cruises steadily on the main sea lane heading north, she just burst into action when she came up to me on the day we met back at The Fowl, and burst into action when she left me, and my goodness if she didn't come bursting back in again now, tonight, and making me leave my childhood home, no, it's beyond understanding, I think and Eline says that the two of us will never be free of each other and I say that it certainly seems like she's right about that

Yes now we'll go home to my house, she says

and I don't say anything

Now you and I will live together again, she says

Yes, how we did before, she says

and I can't think of anything to say

Now we can live together, Frank, you and me, she says

and I understand what she's saying and I understand that what I want or don't want doesn't matter, it's Eline who's making the decisions, now just like before, now as always, whatever I might think and whatever I might say doesn't count for anything, yes, that's how it was, and that's how it is, and that's how it's going to keep on being, I think

It's not the worst place to live, Vaim, you'll like it there, she says

and I think that now I'm going to live in Vaim, clearly that's decided already

There's plenty of fish in the Vaim Fjord, and out in the ocean of course, she says

You can fish and I can keep house, she says

The man I lived with for all those years, Jatgeir, he always had a job, but he also did a lot of fishing, so we always had all the fish we needed, she says

and then there's silence

Did he have a sjark, I say

No, he went to work, he had a motorboat, she says

And what was his motorboat's name, I say

Eline, she says
Was she named after you, I say
Well, she says
But it was already called Eline when we met, she says
Same as my sjark, I say
Yes, well, she says
Yes, I say

and then there's a long silence, and Eline sits there on the chair on the starboard side in the wheelhouse and looks straight ahead and I follow along on the chart and steer by the navigation lights in the water and head north

It won't be long till we're there, she says
Yes you'll have to show me where to go, I say
Yes, okay, she says
It's in The Bay behind the headland you can see up there, she says

and she points

You can just see the cairn on the tip of the headland, she says
It's called just The Headland, she says
And the bay is called just The Bay, she says
Yes, I say

and then we sit there not saying anything

Yes, just think, it's you and me again, she says
We were meant for each other, she says
I just didn't realize it, she says
And then all those years went by, she says
So Jatgeir's motorboat was also called Eline, I say
Yes, she says
Jatgeir's a good name, I say
His real name was Geir, but everyone called him Jatgeir, she says
And he died this past spring, she says
My condolences, I say

Hmph, my condolences, she says

and we steer around The Headland and I see the motorboat Eline lying moored to a big red buoy, and then there's a dock, and back behind the pier is a boathouse, and then I see a white farmhouse on the hill behind the boathouse

That's where you'll live now, Eline says

and she points at the house and I don't say anything

You're not saying anything, Eline says

No, I say

It's a nice place, she says

Yes, I say

and I tie up at the dock and Eline climbs onto land and I throw her the aft mooring line first and then the stern line and the fenders are already out, Eline got them out in plenty of time before we pulled in, and then Eline, my boat, was safe and sound, and the motorboat Eline was moored safe and sound to its buoy and I take the painting of the jakt Matilde and hand it to Eline and I pick up my suitcase and climb out onto the dock and I see Eline disappear around the corner of the boathouse and then I see her come into view around the corner

You need to come on now, Frank, she says

and she's sticking to the name Frank, I think, there was so much talk about Frank and Frank-Olaf and Olaf-Frank and about Frenka or Olaf-Frenka or whatever back in Sund, but then it stopped and my name for all of Sund and to everyone I knew and everyone who knew me was Olaf again, just Olaf

Come on now Frank, she says

and I walk towards Eline carrying my suitcase and then we go up to the little white house and I think yes, yes, there are so many things now

Hurry up, Frank, she says

Yes okay, I say

and all that time we lived together, right up until a few months ago when she suddenly died, I found her dead in the bed next to me, and she must have been feeling bad for a while, because more than once and over the course of many years she'd talked about wanting to be buried next to Jatgeir and as far as I was concerned that was good and fine and totally appropriate of course, but then someone named Elias died, someone that to tell the truth I had only seen a couple of times at The Vaim General Store and had never talked to, but he had been Jatgeir's best friend, Eline had said, and then he was buried next to Jatgeir, and when Eline heard that yes she said that the grave needed to be opened and the coffin taken out and buried somewhere else, because that grave was her grave, Elias that miserable prayerhouse person had taken her grave, but of course everyone said that Elias had to be left in peace and that's why, when Eline died, I arranged it so that she would be buried as close to Jatgeir as possible, and that meant next to Elias too, so that's how it happened, and obviously I followed Eline's wishes, it said and says Josephine on her tombstone, not Eline, and when the tombstone was done and placed I felt strongly and clearly that there was nothing more for me in Vaim, no reason to stay there, so I packed my suitcase again with my Icelandic jumper, my suit and white shirt, tie and nice shoes, that I had only used once, and that was for Eline's funeral, and with the suitcase in one hand and the painting of the jakt Matilde in the other I got on board the sjark Eline and set out, heading south, and now I knew the way very well, because I had gone and looked in on the house and boathouse in Sund rather often, I can't exactly say that Eline liked these trips of mine to Sartor, to Sund, but she put up with them, I think sitting here in my living room here in Sund, on Sartor, in my childhood home, and looking down at the sjark Eline lying prettily moored to the dock and even though I'm now in my seventy-fifth year, and even though I've thought about Eline and me for all these years, I've never come up with any explanation other than that everything was strange, and I'd even thought that that's what my tombstone should say – All was strange – but I've decided that I should stick with a simple cross, I've decided I want just a cross on my tombstone, I don't have any children or heirs and I was thinking I would bequeath everything I own to The Sund Prayerhouse, I've never been especially religious, but when you've lived your whole life on the sea, yes, then you probably become kind of religious, in a way, but I changed my mind and decided against that, it would probably attract too much attention and the people in Sund would start to think that I was secretly a prayerhouse person, so I've written a will leaving everything I own to The Vaim Prayerhouse, and to make sure that it would say Olaf on my tombstone I wrote down that that's what my tombstone should have, a cross and then Olaf

This book is printed with plant-based inks on materials certified by the Forest Stewardship Council®. The FSC® promotes an ecologically, socially and economically responsible management of the world's forests.
This book has been printed without the use of plastic-based coatings.

The authorized representative in the EEA is eucomply OÜ, Pärnu mnt 139b-14,
11317 Tallinn, Estonia.
hello@eucompliancepartner.com
+337 576 90241

Fitzcarraldo Editions
133 Rye Lane
London, SE15 4ST
Great Britain

Copyright © Jon Fosse, 2025
Originally published as *Vaim* by Det Norske Samlaget in 2025
Translation copyright © Damion Searls, 2025
Published by agreement with Winje Agency A/S, Norway
Originally published in Great Britain
by Fitzcarraldo Editions in 2025

The right of Jon Fosse to be identified as the
author of this work has been asserted in accordance with
Section 77 of the Copyright, Designs and Patents Act 1988.

ISBN 978-1-80427-182-7

Design by Ray O'Meara
Typeset in Fitzcarraldo
Printed and bound by Pureprint

All rights reserved. No part of this publication may be
reproduced, stored in a retrieval system or transmitted
in any form or by any means, electronic, mechanical,
photocopying, recording or otherwise, without prior
permission in writing from Fitzcarraldo Editions.

fitzcarraldoeditions.com

Fitzcarraldo Editions